PENGUIN BOOKS

SHE WHO DEVOURS

Bea Bustamante is a schoolteacher by day and a fantasy author by night. After graduating with a degree in Communication from Ateneo de Manila University in 2019, she briefly dipped her toes into the advertising world as an account manager, before realizing her true calling as an educator. Currently, she is finishing her professional teaching certification programme at the University of the Philippines.

She is also a songwriter and musician, occasionally releasing music under the stage name 'Beabu'. She lives in Laguna, Philippines, with her husband. *She Who Devours* is her first novel.

When not teaching or writing, Bea can be found sharing her literary adventures with the BookTok community. Find her at @beabustawrites.

ADVANCE PRAISE FOR *SHE WHO DEVOURS*

'Laden with hair-raising twists, fun characters, and gorgeously eerie imagery, *She Who Devours* is an incredible romp through a rich world proudly steeped in Filipino folklore. Bea Bustamante's prose is electric, her imagination limitless, her talent for creating sparkling chemistry unmatched. This is one of the most delightful and intriguing fantasies I've ever had the pleasure of reading!'

—Thea Guanzon,
author of *The Hurricane Wars*

'*She Who Devours* is filled with action, heartache, family history, fantasy, and my favourite: Filipino folklore. Though set in an imaginary world, this page-turning story clearly draws from Filipino mythology, making my Pinay heart sing. The adventure of reluctant heroine Maya is made all the more impactful by the culture it is rooted in. A big plus for me was the will-they-won't-they tension between Maya and the very intriguing, very cute Aga. I can't wait to read more about these two—and the colourful cast of characters—in the second instalment of *She Who Devours*.'

—Ines Bautista-Yao,
author of *My Lola's Love Letters*

'*She Who Devours* casts a spell. Bea Bustamante has a rare gift for layering folkloric resonance with contemporary relevance. Mythical Filipino creatures are brought to life not as relics from quaint tales but as living, breathing reflections of both personal and societal conflicts. The book's power lies in its balance of intimacy and scope.

Its battles are as gripping as the quiet moments of care and connection. Beneath the folkloric fantasy lies a profound meditation on legacy, identity and the weight of history. A masterwork on myth and memory.'

—Russell Molina,
author of *Sixty-Six*

'Packed with action, romance, and so much heart, *She Who Devours* is everything I've always wanted to read in a fantasy book inspired by my country's mythology. Bea masterfully weaves modern storytelling techniques and tropes, all the while staying true to and respectful of her roots. Like the Bakunawa, this book is a force to be reckoned with—definitely essential reading for Philippine modern fantasy!'

—Mica De Leon,
author of *Love On The Second Read*

'*She Who Devours* is a fantasy novel that draws heavily from Filipino history. Maya Halili is ripped from what she hopes will be the beginning of her academic career and thrust into a hidden world of monsters, mysterious healers, a family secret, and the possibility of love amid a brewing movement to take down not just the evil spirit that has made its way back into the world, but also the oppressive colonial government that has Maya and her people under its thumb. It's a fascinating look at the life of an unwilling hero and what keeps her moving forward despite the ever-mounting costs. The last chapter, in particular, gave me chills!'

—Yvette Tan,
author of *Seek Ye Whore and Other Stories*

'For her debut novel, *She Who Devours*, Bea Bustamante reimagines the Philippines during colonial times—except this time, babaylan and mythological creatures exist. While the book fits neatly into the well-loved romantasy genre (and what an impressive debut it is!), what sets it apart is its horror elements. Bustamante knows how to create tension and write unsettling scenes that genuinely creeped me out. *She Who Devours* is a welcome addition to the growing collection of Filipino fantasy novels. The book left me ready to devour more of Bustamante's works.'

—Koji Arsua,
content creator (@kojireads)

SHE WHO DEVOURS

Bea Bustamante

PENGUIN BOOKS
An imprint of Penguin Random House

PENGUIN BOOKS

Penguin Books is an imprint of the Penguin Random House group of companies whose addresses can be found at global.penguinrandomhouse.com

Published by Penguin Random House SEA Pte Ltd
40 Penjuru Lane, #03-12, Block 2
Singapore 609216

Penguin Random House SEA

First published in Penguin Books by Penguin Random House SEA 2026

10 9 8 7 6 5 4 3 2 1

ISBN 9789815323658

Typeset in Adobe Caslon Pro by MAP Systems, Bengaluru, India

www.penguin.sg

To Papa,
whose stories filled my heart and shaped my soul.
Until we see each other again.

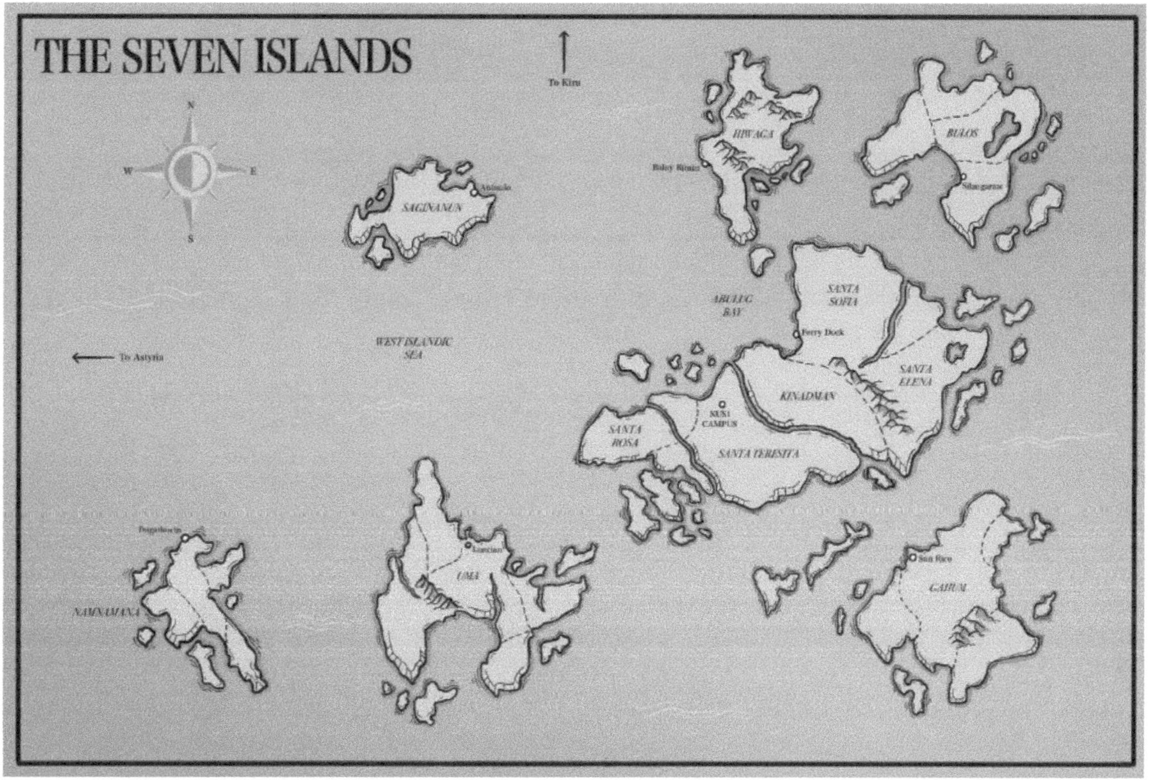
THE SEVEN ISLANDS
To Kiru
N
W
E
S
HIWAGA
BULOS
SAGINANUN
ABULUG
BAY
SANTA
SOFIA
Ferry Dock
WEST ISLANDIC
SEA
To Astyria
SANTA
ELENA
KINADMAN
NUSI
CAMPUS
SANTA
ROSA
SANTA TERESITA
UMA
GAHUM
NAMNAMANA

Prologue

She was coming for them.

They ran screaming from their homes, armed to the teeth with their spears and shields, yet in their hearts they knew that these would not defend them in the end.

She would come for them and destroy their world, and they would have no choice but to watch.

She was wider than the largest tree and longer than the deepest river. Her scales were as dark as the shadows of the forest, until the light of the last moon revealed their brilliant silvery emerald. She swirled around the roots of the trees and skimmed the surface of the waters as she made her way through the world, searching for what she was denied.

She had risen from the sea with a terrible roar, her sorrow driving her to madness as she flew across the lands, searching for something to swallow it away. She left a path of destruction in her wake, levelling entire groves of trees, draining lakes down to their sediments, tearing villages apart with the flick of her tail.

They did not think she would come again.

Kaylahon had warned them all. She had gone straight to their datu, pleading for him to listen to her each night, to look outside and see that their seven moons had now been diminished to just one.

They had not believed her the first six times.

Now, as the last moon stood strong in the sky, she was coming.

She would take from those who had taken from her.

Her body twisted up into the sky as her jaw unhinged to swallow the first moon. They cried out in fear and despair, begging her to spare their last moon, but their pleas did not rise high enough into the sky for her to hear or care. She circled around it, widening the gaping hole of her mouth. They could do nothing but watch in horror as their world slowly plunged itself into darkness.

They called her Bakunawa: She who devours.

Part I

Chapter 1

There was blood.

Maya rolled up her right pant leg to reveal an angry red gash blooming on her calf and cursed under her breath. The pages of her research were strewn across the steps of Jorge Hall, the ink smudging slightly against the concrete.

She was late.

The other students and staff hurrying up and down the steps didn't so much as spare a glance at her as she stood up with a wince and hastily picked up her slightly crumpled papers, eyeing the dark smudges with disdain. She silently admonished past Maya for deciding to wear leather boots instead of her normal Mary Janes for once and thundered her way up to the top of the steps and through the hall's main lobby. She spared a quick wave at the building's lobby guard before launching herself up another flight of stairs to the second floor.

At the entrance to the faculty centre for Humanities, Maya took a deep breath, ran her hands down her pink dress one more time, and pushed the door open. Inside, she was greeted by the welcoming breeze of the extremely cold air-conditioning set way below the university standard. The heat from outside combined with her sprinting had turned her curly hair into a large pouf. She didn't need a mirror to see it. The torturous island humidity made sure of it.

Over the edge of the desk, she spotted a black-haired bun streaked through with grey. She silently cursed again before plastering on the most professional-looking smile she could muster.

'Good afternoon, Mrs Abad,' Maya greeted her as warmly as she could.

Mrs Abad didn't look up from the stack of paperwork she was working on. 'I'd say it's a little late for a good afternoon, don't you think, Ms Halili?' She signed off on a memo with an annoyed flick of her pen.

Maya winced slightly. *Why couldn't Ms Santos be here instead?* 'Good evening, then. I understand that it's past the regular consultation hours, but I need to see Dr Manalo about the collection of references she requested. Would it be possible for me to slip in really quickly to see her?'

Mrs Abad glanced irritably at the clock on the wall behind her before turning back with a frown on her face. 'I'm afraid it's just like you said, Ms Halili. It's past consultation hours. Maybe you should have thought of that before you came in here fifteen minutes after it ended.'

Maya grit her teeth. 'Mrs Abad, I'm not a student any more, remember?'

After graduating at the top of her class last year, Maya's time at the National University of the Seven Islands was now split balancing her one Islandic History lecture and impossibly long hours at the university library, gathering resources and doing supplementary research for her mentor, Dr Manalo. She took pride in the fact that she was the youngest lecturer to ever be accepted at NUSI. Mrs Abad's condescending smile told her that the woman did not care.

'I highly doubt that Dr Manalo would be willing to see you at this hour. Come back tomorrow.' She turned around in her swivel chair, signalling that she was done with the conversation.

'I assure you that Dr Manalo would really appreciate receiving these references regardless.' Maya lifted up her leather satchel high enough for the woman to see that it was threatening to snap at the buckles. 'I have a lot of them,' she paused, 'and they're heavy.'

Mrs Abad leaned in, gesturing for her to come closer. She cupped a hand around her mouth, beckoning Maya to listen.

'I don't care.'

'Mrs Abad, please!'

Mrs Abad took off her glasses and looked at Maya squarely. 'There is no point in setting consultation hours if people are not going to honour them. Dr Manalo is a very busy woman, and probably getting ready to go home. As should you. Good evening, Ms Halili.'

Maya bit her lip. She eyed the pair of wooden swords displayed on the wall under the clock and wondered how heavy they would be if she decided to wield them against unassuming secretaries.

'Obstruction of justice,' she muttered.

'Excuse me?' Mrs Abad looked up sharply.

'I hear a staff member preventing their colleague from doing their required work is against the rules, according to the human resources office.'

Mrs Abad rolled her eyes so hard it looked like she was going to bust a vein. 'Sure.'

'I'm sure Mr Singson is always on the lookout for cases like that.'

'Who's obstructing justice?' a third voice chimed in from the hallway on the right.

A tall, slender woman emerged from the harsh hospital-white light of the hall, green glasses perched on the tip of her nose and black hair gathered in a loose low bun. She sauntered up to the front desk and smiled knowingly at Maya, who could do nothing but stare in admiration.

Veronica Manalo was everything Maya felt like she should be. She was young for a professor, but she was recognized nationwide as the leading expert on pre-colonial Islandic folklore and literature. She burst into the academic scene only a few years ago, and she'd been considered a brilliant mind in the field ever since. The old scholars in the field questioned her quick rise in recognition, even openly discredited her at conferences, but it didn't stop her from securing a highly coveted position in the country's leading university.

When Maya had found out that she was also the moderator of the university paper, *The Archipelago Press*, she had jumped at the chance to be a contributor in her first year at NUSI, all in the hopes of becoming her mentee. Maya hoped that if she worked hard enough, she could earn her place in the field of Island studies and be as deserving of it.

'Dr Manalo,' she pleaded, 'I completely understand that it's a little late in the evening, but I have the resources you asked for. The important ones.'

Her mentor pursed her lips in thought. 'I'm afraid Mrs Abad is right, my dear,' Dr Manalo said. 'It's a little late.' Mrs Abad nodded knowingly in agreement, giving Maya a sneer.

'Lucky for you though, my driver is stuck in traffic. I've got about thirty minutes to spare.' The sound of clicking heels shook Maya from her one-sided staring contest with Mrs Abad. Dr Manalo was already halfway down the hall, beckoning her to follow. She quickly gathered herself and followed, but not before she turned around to throw a very satisfactory wave back at the faculty secretary.

'Veronica!' Mrs Abad huffed, the irritation crystal clear in her voice. 'Consultation hours are over!'

'I'm very much aware, Anna,' Dr Manalo said over her shoulder with a wink, 'but I'd hate for us to be complicit in the obstruction of justice.'

Chapter 2

The only thing standing between Aga Kaneko and freedom was the tower of papers stacked on the desk before him. He stared it down with as much hatred he could muster, which wasn't a lot, considering that he had willingly volunteered to do this.

'It is almost as if I can hear your thoughts all the way from here, Mr Kaneko. Less thinking, more recording,' Dr Tolentino grumbled from behind the mountain range of papers and textbooks on his own desk. Aga rolled his eyes and bit back a smile, a wave of fondness washing over him.

Dr Wilfredo Tolentino was a reedy, irritable old man whose moustache tips extended past the outline of his jaw. His white, wiry hair framed his wrinkly face like an electrocuted lion's mane, which in Aga's opinion further contributed to the professor's terrifying aura.

Aga's eyes had nearly fallen out of their sockets when the university's longest tenured professor and leading expert on Island linguistics shuffled to the front of his classroom on his first day of class as a student, and a confusing mix of awe and terror took hold of him. He had jumped at the chance to be the old man's student assistant, despite knowing he would have to fight off a hundred other Linguistics programme students for the highly coveted position. Perhaps he did have to spend most of his time poring over ancient texts in long-dead languages to keep up with his professor, but it was worth it.

Four years and ten thousand papers later, Aga was still at Dr Tolentino's office every other day until the late evenings, helping him sort through essays and record grades. Being a part-time lecturer was difficult, but not impossible. He hated to admit it, but he sometimes enjoyed Dr Tolentino's company.

There was no one else on campus who would willingly speak to him in Kiruvian without throwing him suspicious looks anyway.

It didn't take much. Islanders needed only to hear his name and see his almond eyes for them to sense what he was. *Who* he was.

Five years since he came to the Seven Islands. Five years of learning as much history, as much culture, as many local languages as he could. He thanked his gods for his affinity to pick things up quickly.

He barely spoke Kiruvian now. It had been so long since he had been back.

Dr Tolentino didn't seem to care though, which was partly why Aga had fought so hard for this position. Never mind the fact that the old man's eyesight and hearing were deteriorating at a much quicker pace than everyone expected. The last time Aga had walked into Dr Tolentino's office, his professor continued to sit perfectly still and relaxed on his armchair, reading his book like no one was in the room. It was only when Aga had started flailing his hands five inches away from Tolentino's face that he noticed him. It was a miracle, albeit a little suspicious, that the university still allowed him to lecture.

Aga took off his glasses and gently set them on the table before rubbing hard at his eyes. When was the last time he had slept?

The Islandic words were swimming on the paper in front of him, and he could feel the beginning of a pounding headache in his temples. Tonight was one of those nights where he felt a touch of regret for taking on more work than was necessary.

A wheezing sigh came from behind the stack of textbooks, sending a cloud of dust up into the air. 'Mr Kaneko, we have spent enough time together for me to know when you are ready to go home.'

Aga huffed, forcing himself to continue scribbling on the professor's grade ledger. The '84' marked in red ink started doubling in his vision. 'Just a few more papers to go, Doc. Don't worry about it.' Gods only knew these papers wouldn't be properly recorded until he came back the day after tomorrow.

'I will not be liable for my research assistant's pending loss of consciousness in my office. Go home, boy.' The thud of a book being closed. 'Those papers won't check themselves until you come back. The Maker knows I can't.'

Aga put his glasses back on with a heavy sigh. 'I've got it, Doc. You said these papers need to be distributed in your class tomorrow morning.'

Aga heard a laboured groan before spotting the tips of Tolentino's white hair peeking out from behind the books. 'Don't make me kick you out of this office. I'll do it. With my good leg, too.'

Aga let out a surprised laugh before leaning back in his chair, the bones in his back cracking down his spine like a string of firecrackers. 'All right, you win. But only because my wrist is starting to cramp.' He tidied up the remaining papers on his side of the desk and placed a green-grey rock that he'd been using as a paperweight on top of the stack. 'How are you getting home?'

A scoff from behind the books again. 'None of your business. Good night, Mr Kaneko.'

Aga felt another laugh bubbling in his chest as he grabbed his jacket off the rack and swung the office door open. Mrs Abad was notoriously strict with the people coming in and out of the faculty centre, even the part-time lecturers, and he wasn't in the mood for another scolding.

Voices carried down the long hallway of faculty offices as Aga shrugged his jacket on. As he rounded the corner, he spotted Dr Manalo walking down the hallway, her green glasses reflecting against the fluorescent lights.

'Good evening, Doc Manalo,' he greeted her with a polite smile and gave a quick bow.

Dr Manalo smiled back with a nod. 'Hello, Aga. Always so proper. Did Wilfredo finally let you out early for a change?' she called out before opening the door to her office.

Aga was about to say that no, he actually had to fight the old man to let him stay, but the words caught in his throat when a flash of pink and a head of dark curls rounded the corner.

Maya Halili was in the hallway with him, and now his night was officially ruined.

Chapter 3

'Evening, Halili.'

Aga Kaneko towered over Maya in the hallway, his jet-black hair falling into his condescending brown eyes. The smell of leather flooded her senses before she spotted his worn jacket draped over his shoulders. That stupid jacket. *Who wears a leather jacket on a tropical island?* Unbearable, stuck-up fools like Aga Kaneko, apparently.

'Kaneko.' Maya narrowed her eyes at him, hands fisting at her sides as she stood as tall as possible. It didn't matter that the top of her head barely touched his shoulders. She would not be intimidated.

'Are you stalking me, Halili? You really need to find a better hobby.' He crossed his arms in front of him, a smirk playing on his lips. 'It's not going to help you.'

'You're not important enough for me to stalk.' She rolled her eyes. 'Now, please move out of my way.'

Aga remained rooted in his spot, his smirk breaking out into a full-on condescending smile. 'Sorry, I only listen to full-time faculty members.' He bent down to be eye level with her, his brown eyes burning a hole through her. 'And I don't see any full-timers in front of me.'

Maya clenched her fists so hard she felt the skin of her palms breaking. 'That's funny. Neither do I.'

The School of Humanities had one full-time faculty position opening at the start of the incoming semester next month. If it came down to Maya and any other research assistant, she would've easily taken it.

But this was Aga Kaneko. Annoyingly brilliant, frustratingly charismatic, and absolutely abhorrent Aga Kaneko, the darling of Dr Tolentino, the Kiruvian slacker who, despite knowing only a handful of words in Islandic as a first-year student, somehow proved his worth and graduated second in their class right behind Maya. She hated to admit it, but it had been a close call. It was always a close call between the two of them.

Aga shrugged. 'For now. Sorry in advance, by the way. I'll make sure to send you a thank you card when I sign that full-timer contract next month.'

Maya scoffed in his face. 'Not with that late clock-in record you won't. How many months has it been since we started? Six? And you've been late how many times now?' She made a show of counting on her fingers. 'Twelve?'

'How nice of you to keep track. See, you're already so good at administrative stuff. You'd be a perfect assistant.' The corners of his mouth lifted up even higher. 'I'll put in a good word for you. Maybe I'll even take you under my wing.'

Maya grimaced at the idea. 'No, thanks. I'd hate to deal with all the backlog you'll accumulate from your less than desirable work ethic.'

'I'd say my work ethic leaves much to be desired,' Aga said confidently.

Maya snorted. 'Gods, that's exactly my point,' she deadpanned. 'That level of unchecked laziness is unbecoming of a future faculty member.' Maya took a few steps back and gave Aga a sickly-sweet smile. 'Also, you should work on your Kinadmani while you're still here. It's getting a little rusty.'

'And why are you here?' Aga scoffed. 'Come to submit your half-baked research way past consultation hours again? Dr Manalo had to come save you from Mrs Abad?' He crossed his arms over his chest. 'I'm not the only one with flaws I need to work on. At least I acknowledge that I have them.'

'How dare you.' Maya could feel her left eye twitch. 'I put in a great amount of time and effort in my research. I wish I could say the same for you.'

'Oh, you can, actually.' Aga's eyes narrowed at her. 'I've got a long-tenured professor to vouch for me.'

'And I've got the newest brilliant mind in Island studies to vouch for me,' she spat back.

'Right. Good luck with that.' Aga gave her a dazzling smile before patting her gently on the shoulder.

'I guess we'll just have to wait and see next month, won't we?' she challenged.

'Careful now, Halili. It almost sounds like you *enjoy* competing with me.'

'It's not a competition if someone's clearly in the lead, Kaneko.' She laced every syllable in his last name with venom. 'And I assure you it's definitely not you.'

Maya spun around on her heel and left him standing in the hallway.

Chapter 4

Stepping into Dr Manalo's office was a fever dream.

Potted plants were strewn around every available surface, situated in between large volumes of special edition encyclopaedias and textbooks. Small artifacts collected from various research trips sat scattered all over, with the larger ones grouped together on the desk. The windowsill was overcrowded with bits and bobbles, all of which reflected off of the sunlight coming in through the large window. The smell of sea salt wafted from the candle lit on top of the desk. The room was white and boxy, just like every other tenured professor's, but it looked like she had actually taken time to make it *hers*.

'You're lucky I was on my way to the pantry, otherwise I wouldn't have been able to rescue you from Mrs Abad's wrath.' Dr Manalo sat in her leather swivel chair behind her desk with an amused look on her face.

Maya breathed out a nervous huff. 'I'm so sorry. I know I should've come in earlier, and now it's late and . . .'

'Maya.' Dr Manalo held up her hand to stop her. 'It's fine. I understand that you have many other responsibilities, and I appreciate you taking the time to visit me at this late hour.'

A sigh of relief escaped Maya, and she relaxed in her chair a little. 'Thank you.'

She reached for her satchel and pulled out a bunch of papers held together with a thick rubber band. 'Here are the references you asked for. I found some passages on pre-colonial religious rituals in the newest acquisitions added to the Island history section.' She ran a finger down the smooth white paper in front of her. 'Most of them date back to over five hundred years ago. There isn't much else dated from the past three hundred years, but you already knew that.' Maya smiled sheepishly.

Dr Manalo smiled sadly. 'Yes, it's a shame, really.'

After the country of Marin had taken the Seven Islands by force three hundred years ago, the Marinese had banned the practise of the Islanders' pre-colonial religions and burned almost every trace of their rituals. The Islanders who pledged allegiance to the Marinese's god, the Maker, were spared. The ones who didn't never lived to tell the tale. It made Island studies a particularly difficult area of research.

'No matter, this will do fine.' Dr Manalo reached over her desk and collected the pile of papers from Maya's hands. 'I'll look at these resources over the weekend and see what I can incorporate into my lectures.' She eyed Maya, a mischievous smile playing on her lips. 'That's not all you have though, is it?'

Maya nodded, pulling out a thick binder notebook from her satchel. 'I know I'm not part of *The Archipelago Press* any more, but I couldn't help but look into what's been happening recently.'

She flipped her notebook open and quickly skimmed over her hastily written notes. 'The recent activity in Santa Teresita has put everyone on high alert. I took the liberty of interviewing some members of the student body about any suspicious activity they've seen around the campus. Most of them have had some unlucky run-ins with Astyrian soldiers patting them down or cornering them for questioning, but a few have reported seeing a group of three or four individuals hanging around the back alleys of Remedios and Loyola near the harbour. The residents of Remedios have described them as . . .' her brows furrowed at her own indecipherable writing, 'street urchins.' She cleared her throat. 'From the far-flung provinces, so they say. Some reported seeing them as far back as a month ago, but no one has seen their faces.'

Dr Manalo pursed her lips. 'So, they're completely anonymous to the public?'

'So far, yes.' Maya looked back down at her notes. 'But people are talking. They've also reported seeing and experiencing strange things happening around Santa Teresita. Minor earthquakes that only affect people from one building. Sudden downpours that only last a few seconds on one street. Towers made of flames that shoot up into the sky.' She looked up at her mentor. 'Islanders think it's a sign of the end times. A small population theorized that it could be a group of Old World believers that are practising rituals in the city.' She closed her notebook abruptly. 'Even if it's outlawed.'

Dr Manalo hummed. 'And the Astyrians are okay with it?'

'Oh, the Astyrians are livid.' Maya chuckled. 'I overheard some drunk soldiers talking about it at a bar on my way home. They think it's an undercover guerilla group sent from one of the stronghold islands, like Namnama or Saginanun. They're planning on making an example of them somehow. You know how the Astyrians are.'

After the Marinese had lost in the Western War twenty years ago, they had struck a financial agreement with another western country looking to create another military base in the East. Astyria was a young and ambitious country and had been the first to reach out to Marin as soon as they caught wind of their plans. Without the Islanders' knowledge, Marin and Astyria had signed a treaty for the peaceful turnover of the Seven Islands to the Astyrians, all for the small price of twenty million talukap.

Maya was a child when the Astyrian flag came marching down her street, accompanied by several foot soldiers and a gigantic, metallic beast that groaned under its own pressure, shaking the concrete underneath her feet. Astyrians rode on top of it and inside it, their pale faces and transparent-looking hair turning red in the sun as they waved at the crowds of hopeful Islanders. They waved their flag, shook hands with the people on the streets, and promised a new dawn had arrived on the Seven Islands. Astyria had called it *benevolent assimilation.*

That was twenty years ago. Things had turned out differently.

Dr Manalo nodded approvingly. 'This is excellent investigative work, Maya.'

Maya beamed at the praise before asking, 'Do you think you can use it for *Archi*'s next issue?'

The professor sighed, clasping her hands together as she leaned back in her chair. 'You know that I have greatly appreciated all of your contributions to *The Archipelago Press*. I will not deny that this particular story is of great concern to the NUSI community.' She paused, leaning her elbows on the hard wood of her desk. 'But the Astyrians will not be happy when they catch wind of a university paper eavesdropping on private conversations between soldiers. They most certainly will do something about it.'

Maya swallowed back the anxious bile rising in her throat. She knew what it meant to publish this story. She would be tagged as a disruptor of peace, a dissident who would be taken to Fort Wallace and mysteriously disappear. The Astyrians took great care of their public image. In the last ten years, they had successfully positioned themselves as the saviours of the Seven Islands.

But Maya knew better.

'People need to know.' She imagined herself being approached by an Astyrian soldier and being forcibly dragged into a military jeep in the shadows. 'Islanders deserve to know.'

Dr Manalo gave her a sympathetic smile. 'I don't think we'll be able to print this until an official police report is released to the public, if they ever will release one.' She reached across the desk and tapped Maya's hand in a soothing motion. 'I'm afraid I can't risk putting you in danger with the Astyrians. You know they've been tagging more and more Islanders as dissidents in the past years. It would be against my duties as your mentor, and against my morals as an educator.' She let out a heavy sigh. 'I don't want you disappearing on me, too.'

The knot in Maya's stomach tightened. 'All right.'

'I still can't believe this is happening. And at NUSI, of all places. Did you know any of them personally?'

'Amanda and I were classmates in first year.' Bright, sunny Amanda Chan, who took pity on her when no one wanted to pair up with her for their Botany lab class. Maya had just moved to Kinadman from her home in Hiwaga, her Kinadmani stiff and her provincial fashion making her stick out like a sore thumb. The local Kinadmani students with their posh accents and sleek clothes eyed her suspiciously, knowing right away that she wasn't one of them. They made snide remarks about her unruly hair and the colour of her skin. They giggled every time she wore the same pair of shoes to school, not knowing it was her only good pair.

'We weren't close, but she was kind to me.' She thought about Amanda's friends and family, who had been putting up missing posters of her all over the university. They fiercely believed she was still alive. 'She didn't deserve it. None of them did.' She felt her eyes getting hot and wet. 'The Astyrians are going too far.'

Memories of Astyrian soldiers standing outside of her home in Hiwaga danced behind her eyes.

'She's innocent!'

'Marikit Halili, you are under arrest for insubordination against the Astyrian military.'

'Let her go!'

'Nanay!'

'Agreed. I haven't seen anything like this in all my years.' Dr Manalo gingerly took off her glasses and placed them on top of her head. 'I sincerely hope that whoever's at work will be brought to justice.' She gave Maya a small smile.

Maya smiled back, wiping away a tear from the corner of her eye before Dr Manalo could see.

Right as her mentor collected the papers from the desk, Maya spotted movement out of the corner of her eye.

Her head snapped to the side, eyeing the shadow cast by the large bookshelf by the window. She squinted, focusing on the darkness before she could see the faint outline standing in it.

Maya leaned back in her chair, careful not to give herself or the shadow away. 'Anyway, thank you again for making time for me. I'm sure your driver must be waiting to take you home by now.'

The shadow in the corner was moving now. It was shaped faintly like a human, but it had no face, save for its black eyes.

A wave of calm resignation washed over Maya. It had been a while since she last saw a spirit. They didn't usually try to distract her in the middle of a meeting, but this one was particularly active.

She couldn't let Dr Manalo know her secret.

It stretched its neck outwards towards Dr Manalo, cocking its head. Maya's eyes widened as the shadow stepped out from the darkness and glided over to stand directly behind her mentor. She shook her head ever so slightly, trying her best to communicate with the shadow. *Behave*, she tried to say. *Not in front of my mentor.*

Dr Manalo waved her hand at Maya dismissively. 'Don't worry about it. Canor can wait.' She tapped the bundle of papers on the desk to align them properly before turning back to Maya. 'Do you need a ride home?'

The shadow grew bigger, as if trying to ward her off. *Don't,* it seemed to say. *Do not accept.*

Maya had long learned to pay heed to the warnings of shadows and spirits, whether she understood their reasons or not. She tried her best to keep her eyes trained on her mentor.

'It's all right,' she replied. 'I can walk.'

As she spoke the words, the shadow receded, as if to say *good girl.* It shrunk to the size of a small dog before slowly moving back to its corner.

'Well, don't walk home alone, okay? *Ingat,*' Dr Manalo warned. *Be safe.*

The shadow melted back into the darkness without a trace.

Chapter 5

Aga stumbled down the steps of Jorge Hall, the soft pounding in his temples making it difficult for him to focus. He groaned, clutching his head in hands, and descended a few steps before sitting down on the last step in front of the building, bending forward in pain. After a few minutes of rocking himself back and forth, he felt the pain start to subside to a dull thud. He really needed to get off work earlier.

A set of soft footsteps approached him from behind, and Aga felt his temples start to throb again, only this time, he knew exactly why.

'Everything all right, Kaneko-oya?' The burly man before him spoke in smooth Kiruvian, his voice deep and gravelly like he had just finished smoking a pack of thirties. His bald head glistened under the moonlight, and for a second, Aga thought he looked like a hard-boiled egg.

'Kenji.' Aga gave him a shallow nod, a sorry excuse for a bow in their culture. 'You're still fairly new around here, so let me reiterate,' Aga spoke informally as he ran his hands through his hair and pulled lightly at the roots. 'You're not supposed to approach or interact with me in public, at any time of the day. Go away.' He waved his hands dismissively at Kenji. 'Go for a smoke break for something.'

Gods forbid that Masaki Kaneko would ever allow his only son to walk around the Seven Islands without someone watching over him. He had already fought his father about it one too many times, and he was tired.

'I'm just making sure, Kaneko-oya. It is my duty to protect you while you are on this mission for your father.' Kenji stood eerily still, his black suit making him blend into the darkness. 'Speaking of, your father has been asking about you. He wants to know when you plan on giving him a call.'

Aga had to hand it to the man. He was getting very good at ignoring Aga's rude behaviour. That was probably why he had lasted longer than any of the other bodyguards that his father had sent from Kiru.

He wanted nothing more from his father. Not his bodyguards or his protection.

Well, not nothing, he realized. That was what landed him in this position in the first place.

A bitter laugh escaped Aga's throat. 'Yeah, yeah. I'll call him tonight. You don't have to remind me.' He stood up from the steps, dusting off the seat of his pants before walking past Kenji towards the main university gate. 'You're dismissed for the night. Go home.' He paused, looking over his shoulder. 'And for gods' sake, change your damn clothes. It's like you're begging people to recognize you as an undercover agent.'

'I'll be nearby if you need anything, Kaneko-oya. You know the number to call,' Kenji called out to him as he walked away. The poor guy. He probably wouldn't last another year if Aga had anything to do with it.

It was already late in the evening, and the main university gate's lights were already turned off. Aga rifled through his bag for the miniature flashlight he always kept on hand for nights like these and flicked it on.

Despite NUSI being comfortably settled in the middle of Kinadman's capital, only the main highway lights of Santa Teresita stayed on throughout the night. Living on a mountainous island meant that there wasn't enough power to generate light for every single street without completely blowing out the generators of the next town.

The concrete on the road back to his apartment was damp with drizzle, and Aga jumped over the tiny puddles that formed on the ground as he replayed the events of the last hour in his mind.

He had no idea how to act around Maya Halili.

It wasn't always so hostile between them. He and Maya were acquaintances at first, always playfully trying to outdo each other with their essays and assignments in their first year. Things changed when their professor assigned them as partners for a literature review project.

Aga hadn't shown up to most of their study sessions. He was so focused on assimilating and securing the student assistant position that he had completely forgotten about all his other responsibilities, including the literature review.

He had locked himself in his apartment to study and emerged an unknown amount of time later.

Aga had shown up to their class only to find out that Maya had asked their professor to work on the literature review on her own, citing irreconcilable differences as the reason why. He found out that he had failed to show up to their study sessions for three consecutive days.

The whole situation had sent Aga into a full-blown panic, causing him to momentarily forget about his guilt and complete his own literature review in time for the deadline. He could still remember Maya's deadly gaze as he handed in his work, complete and on time, and the guilt that crept up his spine. He had received a perfect score. Maya hadn't.

She refused to speak to him for a while after that. She avoided him for the rest of their first year, walking away faster than his eyes could follow as soon as she sensed his presence.

It wasn't like he did it on purpose. It irked him that she had passed judgment on him so quickly without ever hearing his side of things, or that she never gave him a chance to properly apologize. Aga knew he should've tried harder, but in truth, a dark, ugly part of him thought it was humiliating. People around him already looked at him like an exotic animal for the way he looked and the languages he spoke. The younger him didn't have the courage to walk up to a beautiful girl like Maya, much less have a conversation after what he did.

I'm a coward. In more ways than one.

When keeping a low profile didn't exactly work out, Aga realized that he might as well try his best. It turned out that his best was pretty good, almost as good as Maya Halili. Eventually, their shared classes and interests had forced them back into each other's space. They could never truly avoid each other in the end.

It had been years since their falling out, but he still felt that small seed of guilt weighing him down every time he saw her. That, and a damning heat in the pit of his stomach that made him strike, made him say anything to get her to keep talking to him, to keep looking at him, to *notice him.*

She was the smartest person Aga had ever met, her words sharp, her thoughts fascinating and full of depth. Aga thought of the first time they verbally sparred in their undergraduate Island History class, Maya's eyes blazing and her hair curling wildly behind her as she pointed out all the reasons why the Seven Islands of Old had all the elements necessary to develop on its own without colonization. He had watched her in awe, wondering how such a woman could exist and how he had messed up so badly for her to despise him.

He would never know. She would shine as bright as the stars in the night sky, and he would do nothing but watch from afar.

Aga felt the puddle before he heard it. He looked down, seeing that his left boot was now soaked with dirty rainwater. *Great.* Even when she wasn't around, Maya Halili still managed to distract him.

He sighed heavily and brought out the apartment key in his pocket. He knew that the weird pothole that he always stepped in was in front of his building.

'Good evening, Nanay Alma,' he called out to the old lady sitting on the second-floor balcony. The old Islandic woman that was his landlord squinted at him before calling out, 'Hoy, *iho!* Why are you home so late again, *ha*?' She waved her fan at him aggressively. 'Go to sleep!'

Aga walked through the glass door, hitting the tiny golden bells attached to the door frame before running through the tiny lobby and jogging up the steps to the fourth floor, two at a time. 'Goodnight!' he called out to Nanay Alma when he passed the second landing.

In his dark studio apartment, Aga dropped all his stuff on the floor before launching himself onto the twin-sized mattress set up beside the tiny window. He took a few deep breaths, steeling himself for what he was about to do.

He reached out for the telephone beside his bed and dialled.

It rang two times before the person on the other end picked it up.

'Agatzuki. You've kept me waiting.' His father's voice was cold and emotionless, just like the man himself.

'I just got home, tado-oya.'

'Never mind that. You haven't called me in weeks. I'm assuming you have something good for me, so spit it out. What do you have?'

Aga took another deep breath. If Maya knew what he was doing now, she would never forgive him.

It didn't stop him from pulling out the little machine in his pocket and playing back the audio recording from Maya's meeting with Dr Manalo. It was a miracle that they had run into each other again in the hallway. Otherwise, he wouldn't have had any other opportunity to plant the listening device on her. Ever since they graduated, their interactions had lessened.

Aga winced as he listened to her passionately reporting her findings to her mentor, then translated the dialogue into Kiruvian for his father.

'Islanders' dissent against the Astyrians is growing. There has been a string of disappearances in the city. Some are chalking it up to Astyrians' dirty work, others are pinning it on a group of street urchins causing trouble around the dock area. Either way, people are on high alert, and all eyes are on the Astyrians,' he recounted what Maya described to her mentor in detail, careful not to mention her name.

Aga felt his body melting into the mattress. Every time he did this, he felt a piece of his soul crumble.

'Good.' As the right-hand man to General Ito, Masaki Kaneko was a difficult man to please. Aga must have given him exactly what he was looking for. 'Any news about what the Astyrians are planning to do?'

'Haven't heard anything from my sources, but I've observed stricter curfews and rule reinforcements since last month, especially with the disappearances. Something is up, but I can't tell what exactly.'

'Then it seems like our plan will push through sooner rather than later.' His father went silent on the other end of the line.

'All right.' Aga's voice hardened. 'Is that all?'

'That is all,' Masaki confirmed. 'Remember our deal, Agatzuki.'

Information in exchange for freedom, his father had promised. *Do this, and I will cut you loose. I will set you free.*

Away from the expectations and pressures of Kiruvian high society. Away from arranged marriages, inherited positions, and cold, emotionless eyes that always wanted more.

It had been five years since that promise, and he was getting impatient. He was so tempted to throw it all away. Stop the calls to his father, run away with whatever money he had saved up and disappear into thin air.

But he couldn't. *Not yet*, he thought.

His father took his silence as agreement. 'I expect your next call to come sooner than later.' The line went dead.

Aga stared up at the ceiling, the dial tone ringing in his ear.

I'm a coward. In more ways than one.

Chapter 6

'Remind me to never leave for class without eating breakfast.'

Maya leaned back in the pantry chair as she called out to Hanan. Her younger sister stood at the pantry's kitchen counter, cutting up vegetables for the omelette they were going to share.

'I always eat breakfast,' Hanan grumbled as she slivered the onions into thin pieces. The pantry of their women's dormitory was shared amongst all the residents, but that didn't stop Hanan from walking around barefoot in nothing but a laughably oversized t-shirt. She leaned over her chopping board, inspecting the variety of cut vegetables like an overzealous food inspector.

'That's why I said I need *you* to remind *me*.' Maya walked over to Hanan and plucked a slice of raw onion off the board, dropping it in her mouth and narrowly missing Hanan's knife and deathly glare. She blew her younger sister a kiss.

'One of these days, I'm gonna chop off one of your fingers.' Hanan waved her own finger threateningly at Maya as she bounced away. 'On purpose,' she spoke sternly to Maya in their native Hiwagani. Despite Maya being the eldest, Hanan had always acted like the older one.

'You and I both know that you don't mean that,' Maya replied, her Hiwagani quick and impatient. 'Need I also remind you that *you* have a date with Anton Ortiguera at lunch today? He said to meet in front of Perez Hall after your class.' She took the chopping board loaded with vegetables and threw them into the hot pan waiting on the stove, cracking four eggs on the way. After a few minutes of intense stirring, Maya plated the vegetable omelette on a clean plate and placed it haphazardly on the wobbly dining table behind her.

'Oh, gods, you're right!' Hanan sat down on one of the matching wobbly dining chairs and split the omelette in two with her fork, pushing Maya's half towards her and eating hers in one swallow. 'You don't think he'll stand me up, right?'

Maya shook her head and smiled. 'Impossible.'

Hanan smiled. 'You're such a smooth talker. You should put that mouth to good use and go out on a date for once.'

Maya almost choked on her bite of omelette at the thought. She would never speak of it to Hanan, but she couldn't bring herself to go out on a date. Not when she knew deep down what people thought of her. She shot a glance at the dirty mirror hanging beside the pantry refrigerator.

Her untameable curls made her look wild and messy. Her round eyes were an unremarkable shade of dark brown. Her nose had been described by a former teacher as flat and wide. She was short and muscular, and her skin was permanently tan after years of swimming in the sea, right beside their childhood home. It made her look like a child of the Seven Islands, an undiluted legacy of the Old World, and that sort of beauty didn't do well in these times. Not after 300 years of Marinese influence. Not with the Astyrians walking around with pale skin and blond hair.

'Who, me? You know I don't do that sort of thing, Han.'

In contrast, Hanan's hair had a slight wave to it, her skin lighter, her nose bridge a little higher, and her cheeks a perfect rosy flush. She was taller and more slender, and both boys and girls from every year level constantly vied for her attention despite Hanan being only in her second year at NUSI. Hanan was *beautiful.* Maya knew that.

'There's no harm in trying. I'm sure plenty of people would love to get to know you.'

'I highly doubt that.' Maya shook her head.

She also knew what word the city folk used around her. She looked too *native* in their eyes, and therefore undesirable.

'What about that girl in your second year Mathematics class that you said was cute? Lourdes, was that her name?'

Maya rolled her eyes. 'Oh, please. Lourdes Flores is old news. And she doesn't like women like that.' She put both her hands up in the air. 'Let's drop it, Han. I'm not interested in dating, and that's that.'

'Shoot, it's already eight and I need at least an hour and a half to shower and enter my creative genius headspace.' Hanan ignored her and jumped off the dining chair, her feet sliding across the tiled floor. 'I feel like Advanced Sewing is going to drain me of every drop of energy I have today.'

'You'll do fine, Han.' Maya shoved another spoonful of omelette in her mouth. 'You always do.'

'Hmm.' Hanan looked like she was about to say something else, but she shrugged and turned back around to leave. 'Just let me know if you need anything, all right? I'll be back before dinner. Maybe. Actually, it depends. If things go well with Anton Ortiguera, I might not even come back tonight.' She smiled knowingly.

'Hey, don't joke about that.' Maya's eyebrows furrowed in worry. 'Not with everything going on. Come home tonight.'

'All right, I was just kidding.' Hanan stuck her tongue out at her older sister. 'I'll see you tonight.'

'Remember what lola said,' Maya warned.

Hanan waved her away. 'Yeah, yeah. Don't talk to any Astyrians. Keep your head low and your mouth shut.'

'Be serious.'

'I am.' She stood up from her chair. 'I know you're worried. But I'm not going to end up like Nanay.' She paused. 'Or Tatay.'

Maya stopped her chewing. 'Don't say that.'

Hanan raised an eyebrow. 'Maya, it was years ago. It's time we acknowledge it and talk about it like adults.'

'We are talking about it like adults. It's a miracle we even have each other to talk about it with. Gods know

Tatay would have a heart attack if we ever try to bring it up around him.'

'Yeah, well,' Maya rolled her eyes, 'if we ever saw him.'

Danilo Halili was a hardworking man, Maya could admit that much. But ever since their mother passed, their father was a shell of the man he used to be. When the girls came to Kinadman to study, their father moved to a small town in Gahum, found a new job and a solo apartment on his own, and didn't speak to them for months. Fifteen years later, he still barely spoke to them, save for their birthdays. They had learned to grow up without him.

Hanan pressed her lips together. 'I was there too, you know.'

'But I saw it, Hanan,' Maya pressed on. 'I remember.'

Hanan held her gaze for one more second before turning away and sighing. 'Fine. I'll be careful.'

Maya let out a shaky breath. 'Thank you.'

'Ingat. Love you.' Hanan bounded away from the pantry and through the doorway.

'Hmm,' Maya replied, the soft smile on her face fading as she considered her sister's words.

A faint humming sound reverberated in the hallway. Maya cocked her head, listening to it carefully. There were no footsteps sounding against the linoleum floor, no squeak of shoes against the tiles. No other voices echoing in the hallway.

The spirit of the young girl was wandering around the dormitory again.

Maya smiled to herself. The little girl didn't speak, but she hummed the same tune over and over again. Based on her clothes, she seemed to have died a few decades ago during the Marinese period. Maya liked her.

The night her mother was taken by the Astyrians was the night the whispers started.

Maya was scared at first, but no one believed her when she tried to explain it. Her own family chalked it up to trauma and grief from losing their mother. *I understand that you're in despair, child. Let the grief flow out of you.*

Over time, she had learned to live with the initial shock of hearing and seeing spirits around her. These days, coming across a wandering spirit or a curious shadow was a common sight. Apart from Hanan, no one else knew that she could see and hear what she did.

Her mind replayed her younger sister's words. *I'm sure plenty of people would love to get to know you.*

The memory of golden-brown eyes flashed before her, just like it had for the past two nights. She couldn't stop the heat that crept up her cheeks.

Aga Kaneko was the last person in the world she should be thinking about right now. She was absolutely certain that he wasn't thinking about her. Not after the way she talked to him that night.

After their little fallout, Maya couldn't bring herself to speak to him, much less be around him. After he had completely abandoned her during their literature project and left her to do everything on her own, he had shown up on the due date with a completed review and had gotten a perfect score on it. She was absolutely furious with him. *How dare he? How could anyone have the audacity?*

She had foolishly hoped that their shared interest in academics would be the foundation of a friendship, but she was wrong. Aga Kaneko wasn't interested in anything but himself. He was a self-serving scoundrel, and she was right to stay away from him.

Perhaps in another life, she could have appreciated those intelligent eyes and that insufferable smirk.

She shook her head off the stray thought before it could go any further. Thank the gods it never came to that.

She looked up at the wall clock and groaned. She was going to be late to her Island History lecture, which coincidentally, was right before Aga's Introduction to Island Languages lecture. They just so happened to schedule them in the same lecture hall.

She sighed. She would not be free of Aga Kaneko any time soon.

Chapter 7

'Thank you for walking me home.'

Hanan felt the heat filling her cheeks as Anton Ortiguera smiled at her, his long eyelashes fluttering in the cool breeze of the incoming wet season. It was the latter half of the year, and the sky was an unremarkable shade of grey, but to Hanan, it didn't matter. It could start pouring for all she cared.

She wasn't expecting someone like Anton to be interested in her, much less ask her out on a date. Hanan had her fair share of suitors, and she had no qualms about picking out the ones who seemed like a good time.

'It's no problem. We're passing by my house anyway, so I'll head home right after I drop you off.' Anton's hand brushed against hers, and for a split second, she felt a surge of courage. 'Is this okay?' Hanan whispered as she slowly wrapped a pinkie finger around his. She looked at Anton, hoping to see him feel the same rush of excitement she did. 'I'll stop if it's not.'

'Let's go out,' Anton had asked Hanan a week ago. They had been standing in front of Perez Hall right after their class had ended.

Hanan was talking to a group of her friends before she turned around slowly, blinking like a wild animal caught in headlights.

'I'm sorry, I don't mean to assume, but are you talking to me?' Hanan stammered out.

Anton laughed. 'Yes, you. Go out with me.'

The girls behind Hanan giggled and whispered to each other. Hanan tucked a hand behind her back and gestured for them to be quiet. She smiled.

'You're Anton Ortiguera.'

'Yes.'

'Everyone has a crush on you.'

'Yes.'

'But you want to go out with me?'

It was Anton's turn to smile. 'Yes.'

They turned the corner on to Guevarra Street, where the stately homes of Islander diplomats stood towering over the makeshift food cart vendors and peddlers scattered all over, calling to fellow Islanders to sell fresh mangoes, fried bananas artfully wrapped in pandan leaves, and rice cakes sprinkled with brown sugar and coconut shavings. Anton lived in one of those giant mansions and probably saw these things every single day, but the smell of Guevarra was always Hanan's favourite part of walking home.

She turned back to look at Anton, only for her heart to drop.

Anton's face had paled, his round eyes widening in fear. He stopped walking, rooting Hanan in place with him.

'Sorry, I didn't realize we were turning here.' He laughed nervously. 'Must be a force of habit.' His eyes darted around Guevarra Street. There were a few Islanders walking about, but no one was paying them any attention. People passed by them without a second look.

'Don't worry,' Hanan tried, her pinkie tightening around his.

'Hanan, please. Not here.' Anton pulled his hand away, leaving Hanan's cold and empty.

She tried to ignore the sting of rejection in her chest. 'It's just Islanders here. No Astyrians.'

'You don't know that for sure. They could be hiding in some random alleyway.' Anton's eyes darted around them.

'So what?' Hanan asked, feeling irritated now. 'Who cares?'

'You know my father's a diplomat.' He smiled apologetically. 'You understand. Things are complicated.'

'Why would it be complicated?' Hanan asked, a deep pit forming in her stomach.

Anton shrugged. 'Well, you know how it is. The Ortiguera name has been associated with Astyrian diplomatic affairs for years. I have my father's reputation to uphold. I have to be careful with what I say, how I act, and . . .' he trailed off, sighing loudly, 'who I'm spotted with.'

Hanan flexed the hand that Anton had dropped. 'I didn't know you cared about all of that.'

Anton laughed. 'Of course I do. We've been a colony for centuries at this point, it's not like it's anything new.

Whether we like it or not, we're Astyrian property now. That means playing the game.'

Hanan stared at him. 'Do you really think that? That we belong to the Astyrians?' The disbelief made her chest ache. *Not you too, Anton.* 'That they *own us*?'

Hanan had her fair share of conversations like this with her classmates. So many of them were so willing to let go of the past. *Too willing*. They chose to turn a blind eye to what the Seven Islands had suffered and accept their fate.

Anton shrugged. 'Doesn't matter what I think. They're here, and they don't plan on leaving any time soon. Might as well.'

They didn't know what it felt like to have their homes taken from them. They didn't remember.

But Hanan did. She remembered. Her family made sure of it.

'She's innocent!'

'Marikit Halili, you are under arrest for insubordination against the Astyrian military.'

'Let her go!'

'Nanay!'

'But what about all the things you said in debate class?' Hanan demanded. 'Or was that all a lie?'

Anton had the audacity to laugh in Hanan's face. 'Hanan, be serious. You and I both know how difficult it is to pass with Mr Reyes as a professor. I did what I had to do.'

Hanan was speechless. This beautiful boy, the one that had passionately defended the Seven Islands' right to independence, had just destroyed everything Hanan thought he was.

Anton smiled at Hanan, moving a step closer. 'I wasn't making up my interest in you, though. I'd still very much like to see you, Hanan.'

'What do you mean?' Hanan took a step back.

'I just ask that we take a different route and enjoy each other's company in privacy. Your place, preferably.' He winked at her, and Hanan felt the bile rise in her throat.

'I'm sorry.' Hanan took a step back. 'I don't think I can do this.'

It was Anton's turn to stare, his eyebrows pressing together in the centre of his forehead and forming an ugly frown line. 'Oh. Why not?'

Hanan shook her head. 'Thanks for your time. I hope you get home safely.' She turned around, ready to leave him.

'Hanan.' Anton's voice was hard now. 'You're making a mistake.'

She whipped her head back around in surprise. 'What did you say?'

'If you come with me now, I'll make sure you won't regret it,' he countered, his sweet demeanour now gone. 'Say yes to me.'

Hanan balled her fists at her side. 'And if I don't?'

This couldn't be the same Anton Ortiguera that everyone fawned over. This Anton had eyes that glistened with something dark and sinister.

He smiled. 'Try me.'

Hanan took a step forward and jammed a finger in Anton's face. 'You think you're untouchable because your daddy is an Astyrian diplomat? Well, tough luck. I'm not afraid of the Astyrians, I'm not afraid of your father, and

I'm not afraid of *you* either!' She was aware that she was shouting now, but she couldn't help it.

Anton was wrong. Anton was wrong and he was vile, and she wasn't going to let an opportunity to put him in his place slip away.

This wasn't what her mother died for. This wasn't what her family suffered for. She felt the anger rearing its ugly head within her, forcing her to speak.

Anton merely scoffed at her. 'You're telling me you're not afraid of the Astyrians?' His voice was getting louder now. 'You're mad!' He took a step back. 'Wait until my father hears about this!'

'*Tak* the Astyrians!' Hanan cursed at Anton. '*Tak you, and tak them all!*'

The low chatter around them on Guevarra Street faded into silence.

Hanan could hear her laboured breaths and the blood pounding in her temples.

'Hanan,' Anton whispered, his jaw wide open, his eyes wide in equal parts shock and horror.

Hanan took a look around her. Islanders on their side of Guevarra Street stared back at her, clearly close enough to have heard what she said. Some of them mirrored Anton's horrified expression, while others looked at her with quiet affirmation.

'I said what I said.' She raised her chin up high.

'You sure did,' a voice spoke behind her.

The sounds of heavy footsteps and metal clinking against leather filled the emptiness.

'Excuse me, miss.' Astyrian drawl. 'What seems to be the problem here?'

Hanan's hands went cold. She turned around.

Two tall shadows moved out from the alleyway behind her, revealing a pair of Astyrian soldiers. They stalked towards her, their pale eyes glistening against the fading afternoon light.

'Well, look what we have here, Jimmy.' The soldier who spoke had a much heavier accent than the first, his vowels dragging. 'A feast for the eyes if I've ever seen one.' He whistled, making the other one with red hair laugh.

'Good afternoon, sirs.' Behind her, Anton quickly switched to smooth Astyrian. Hanan whipped her head back around, only to see Anton flash the two Astyrian soldiers behind her a dazzling smile. 'My friend and I were just on our way home. My father, Mr Ortiguera, is expecting us.'

'Ah,' the red-haired one said, 'you're Arturo's son. Always forget he has one.' Maya pushed down the satisfactory laugh in her chest at Anton's annoyed face.

The other one with the dirty blonde hair clucked their tongue. 'Now, I don't got no problem with you, son. You run along home now.' A large hand clamped tightly on Hanan's right shoulder. 'I'm gonna need to talk to your pretty friend, though.'

Hanan felt a chill run down her spine. The hand pulled at her shoulder hard, forcing her to spin around. A pale, sunburnt face hidden behind a pair of black sunglasses looked down at her with a smile on its face.

'Anton,' Hanan whispered, but she didn't hear a response.

'Now, you mind telling me what you two young lovebirds were quarrelling about?' The Astyrian soldier took a step forward, forcing Hanan to take three steps back. Her shoulders collided with concrete.

They were inside the alley now, hidden from the eyes of Islanders and fellow Astyrians. Far enough inside for no one to hear them.

The soldier placed an arm over Hanan's head and leaned over her, his hot breath on her forehead.

'Nothing, sir.' Hanan stuttered.

'Now, that's not what I heard. What 'bout you, Clark?' The soldier named Jimmy turned to his companion.

'Nah, definitely not. I sure as hell heard somethin' else.' Clark snickered.

Jimmy turned back to Hanan, the sick smile still plastered on his face. 'Tak the Astyrians, right?' Hanan felt a hot hand grip her hard on her waist. 'Now, that's real funny. Ain't that funny, Clark?'

'Sure is, Jim.'

'How'd you like it if I showed you how to do just that?'

Hanan's skin burned where the Astyrian was touching her. She kept her eyes trained on the pavement below her feet, willing whatever god was out there to *save her. Please,* she begged. *Someone help me.*

Keep your head low, lola had said. *Keep your mouth shut. Don't give them any reason to target you.* She had failed to do either of those things.

I'm sorry, she pleaded. *I'm sorry. I'm sorry.*

'Please.' The sound of her own voice was faint and weak to her ears.

The Astyrian soldier's grip tightened on her dress. Hanan pressed her eyes shut.

She imagined she was back home in Hiwaga. She was with her parents, her lola, and Maya. They were sitting at the dinner table, exchanging stories and listening to the sound of the rain pattering on their makeshift tin roof.

A drop of it fell on the tip of her nose.

Wait.

'What the hell?' the Astyrian named Clark said.

Hanan opened her eyes just in time to see a massive rush of water drop down on Jimmy, completely soaking him from head to toe. The man shouted in surprise as the water came down on him, causing him to swallow mouthfuls of it. He bent over, choking as Clark, who was also soaked, started hitting him on the back to get all the water out.

Hanan stood there, completely confused. *What the tak just happened?*

She slid past the two Astyrians, running out of the alleyway and looking around for an escape route. There was no trace of Anton. He had completely abandoned her.

Other Islanders on Guevarra had moved farther away from them, pretending to be completely oblivious to what had just happened.

A cold hand wrapped around Hanan's mouth and pulled her towards another dark alleyway.

Hanan's muffled screams reverberated against the dirty brick walls on either side of her. She was pushed back against one of them, a cold hand still on her mouth, before she came face to face with her attacker.

She was greeted by a pair of light blue eyes, framed by thick eyebrows. Hanan could see a light-coloured scar in the middle of the attacker's forehead with five points stretched outwards in the shape of a star.

The attacker raised his hand at chest level, his palm facing Hanan. He did not speak, but he stared at Hanan, his eyes asking her a question.

Hanan shook her head, adrenaline pumping through her veins and clouding her vision. She had no idea who this person was or what he wanted. The silent stranger frowned at her, raising an eyebrow and cocking his head to the side.

'Who are you?' she demanded. 'What do you want? Are you with the Astyrians?'

The stranger remained silent before raising his palm up to the sky. Around them, water droplets from the cement beneath their feet slowly rose from the ground. Hanan yelped as they began dancing around them in a circle, forming abstract shapes and diving themselves over and over again behind him. The fading afternoon light shone against them, painting shimmery reflections against the concrete all around them.

Hanan blinked once, then twice, before the pressure on her mouth lifted. She stared at the stranger. His eyes weren't just blue. They were *glowing*.

She blinked a third time. She felt a rush of air whoosh past her. By her fourth blink, the stranger had disappeared.

Chapter 8

By the time Maya made it back to her dormitory, the pounding in her temples had faded to a soft thudding.

She sighed, rubbing at her eyes and groaning.

The spirits were everywhere today.

In her lecture classroom, in the hallway, standing over her in the bathroom, following her around campus like a trail of shadows. She was sure a few of them even followed her all the way home. She didn't usually feel any physical symptoms when she saw the spirits, but the sheer amount of them had caused her vision to blur and her hands to shake, causing her to stumble over the steps to Jorge Hall and stubbing her toe. After that, she decided it was time to go home early.

She dug for her apartment keys in her skirt pocket and blindly stuck it into the lock, tripping over herself on the way inside.

Maya flipped on the lights and sat down on her bed, breathing a heavy sigh. She reached over to her bedside table where the latest letter from their Lola Cora sat, waiting to be read. Her paternal grandmother was a spritely old woman, living all the way back on Hiwaga. She had raised Maya and Hanan on her own after their mother disappeared, and their father had abandoned them. By the time she was ten, Lola Cora had been their sole caretaker.

Maya unfolded the letter in her hands and skimmed over it one more time, her grandmother's words wrapping her in warmth.

Mayari and Hanan,

How are you, my darling girls? I am doing very well, all things considered. Good news! Since you last wrote to me, our mango tree has borne fruit. The fruits are sweet and juicy. It bore so much that I had to give some away to Nena and Benito next door. Otherwise, our entire yard would be covered in them! No need to worry, because I kept enough to make mango sago for you two the next time you visit. Speaking of which, when will you be coming home? Let me know so that I can meet you at the dock. Ulan and I miss you very much. He has been howling at the moon more often these days.

I hope that the two of you are well and safe. Remember to go home early. Keep your head down and your mouth shut. Don't draw any attention to yourself. I have always thought that you two have good heads on your shoulders and a strong inner compass. Let it and the Maker guide you towards safety. Ingat.

Love,
lola

Maya smiled, her grandmother's words and exhaustion seeping into her bones. She grimaced slightly at her use of 'the Maker', wondering where her grandmother had picked that habit back up. Perhaps she was spending too much time with Nena and Benito again.

Ever since the Marinese came to their shores, the Fideist faith had exploded in popularity with the Islanders. Like the majority of the population, Maya had gone to a public school and was forced to practise Fideism alongside her fellow students. Unlike the Old World beliefs, Fideism had one god—the Maker. A male god who created and sustained all. A benevolent, all-knowing being who forgave wrongdoings and loved everyone. Her family, however, still practised old traditions that Fideism never taught them. They still told stories of the Old World gods, still prayed to them every once in a while, and still left offerings of food on their doorstep every Day of Souls. Barely anyone practised the Old World beliefs exclusively now, but to Maya and her family, it was part of their history. Her mother had told them stories of the Old World every night before bed. Right before she disappeared.

She slowly reached out for her notebook and pencil to leave a note for Hanan. She wasn't sure when her younger sister was coming home, so she decided to detail how she was currently feeling and listed down reminders for groceries the next morning, just in case she fell asleep.

She had just managed to write down *eggs* and *bread* before the pencil in her hand began to shake.

She grunted in frustration, trying her best to make the muscles in her hand taut. Her eyebrows furrowed as she concentrated all her force into writing the next few words.

She failed, the pencil continuing to shake. She tried again, only for the pencil to fall out of her hand. She looked down at the words.

Her writing looked like random, indecipherable scribbling. She tore out the page and crumpled it into a ball, trying again on a new one.

She closed her eyes and leaned back on her headboard. Her headache was probably worse than she imagined.

She heard the scribbling before she felt it.

Maya looked up slowly, barely registering the lone sound of a pencil on paper. She felt her hand twitching.

That was before she looked down and noticed the notebook in her lap and the pencil in her hand, moving on its own.

On the page was a name written in a stranger's handwriting.

Mayari.

Cold ice shot up Maya's left arm, freezing her entire body into place.

That was strange. She didn't write that.

She closed her eyes and leaned back on the headboard again, certain she was making things up out of exhaustion.

Her hand was twitching again. The soft scratching of lead on paper filled the room.

Her eyes shot open and looked down at her notebook. The writing had continued on the next line.

Mayari Halili.

Her lungs suddenly felt like they could no longer expand, no longer take in any air to breathe, and her legs stayed frozen in their crossed position as her eyes darted around the room, sheer panic and an overwhelming fear consuming her.

She looked down at the handwriting again. The lettering was sharp and angled, the urgent, dark strokes leaving indentations in the paper.

Am I going insane?

Maya swallowed hard. She had not lost control of her own voice just yet.

'Hello?' she called out in a shaky whisper. She had the wild thought that maybe a spirit had found its way into her room.

She felt a cold gust of wind blow against her in response.

Her throat closed up, feeling cold and dry. The windows and the door were all closed.

The pencil in her hand began to move again, and this time she watched as the words began to form on the page against her will.

She pulled against the invisible force moving her hand across the paper, but it was no use. She was taken.

Her entire body felt like it was aflame. She blinked away the tears forming in her eyes as she fought the invisible force wrapped around her, using her as a vessel for the message they needed her to receive.

She was trapped, and she had no choice but to read what it said.

The force on her hand eased and she dropped the pencil in surprise, letting it clatter to the floor.

The words on the page sent a chill up her spine. It was written in her native Hiwagani.

Your time has come.

Maya let out a bloodcurdling scream before she felt the presence swallow her in darkness.

Chapter 9

Aga was lost.

After his phone call with his father, the guilt had kept him up all night. Memories of their conversations over the last few years replayed over and over again, all of them circling back to Maya. His source and his foundation. The one person who had gotten him to where he was now.

And she doesn't even know. She didn't know anything. He had made Maya an unknowing accomplice to something bigger than the two of them, and it was all his fault.

He had to do something before the guilt ate away at him completely.

Today, while burning his tongue on his hot breakfast *misua,* he remembered. He had a lecture in Room 404 at Ferrer Hall right after hers.

Maya Halili. Today would be the day he would finally try and properly talk to her. Maybe it would ease some of the heaviness in his already heavy heart.

Today he would not be a coward.

After his lecture, he had caught a glimpse of her disappearing into the sea of students crowding the main hallway of Perez Hall. He had tried to catch up with her, only to accidentally elbow a poor girl in the back.

'Sorry!' he called out before seeing the girl's boyfriend look back at him with murder in his eyes. He winced before getting swallowed by the crowd, panic slowly building in his chest.

He finally made it to the end of the hallway, with no Maya in sight. Mid-afternoon sunshine lit the floor tiles through the wooden double doors that led into the courtyard. Aga shielded his eyes as he walked outside, spinning around to look for a lavender dress and a head of dark curls. Nothing.

He spotted a bald man lurking underneath the row of trees on the side of the administrative building and sighed.

Kenji leaned leisurely against a large *kamagong* tree, the spots of sun shining between the leaves and dancing across his plain black polo and chino pants. For once, it actually made him blend in with the rest of the young Islander students, save for the baldness.

Unfortunately, Aga's eyes decided at that moment to lock eyes with him. Kenji's brows furrowed slightly in question, his crossed arms falling to his sides as he stood up straighter, waiting to move in reaction to Aga.

Aga groaned. He had to lose him if he wanted any real chance of finding Maya.

Another large group of dismissed students spilled out into the courtyard, swarming around him. He spared a quick glance at Kenji, who was now slowly moving towards him. Aga allowed himself to be carried by the large group of students into the bustling open cafeteria next door.

Angeles Hall was completely full of students having a late lunch or taking a shortcut to their next class. The smell of fried garlic and fish sauce flooded his senses as he walked quickly past the different food stalls, all serving a variety of his favourite Islandic dishes. Aga's stomach grumbled as he swerved around a girl carrying a plate of lechon kawali, the steam from the meat fogging up the edges of his glasses. *Lunch would have to wait.*

He weaved through the crowd of people silently, ignoring their surprised glances and the occasional stares. He looked back to see Kenji's bald head sticking out from the crowd all the way at the entrance to the cafeteria. *Perfect.*

Aga made a quick turn to the right up the narrow flight of stairs that led to the second floor. He took two steps at a time, careful not to make too much noise on the wooden planks. He landed on the patio roof, where other students were enjoying their lunch under large umbrellas covering the wooden dining tables. A few others were lounging on mats they had strewn across the middle of the floor, eyes closed as they basked in the sunlight.

Aga let out a hasty apology as he stepped over them, speed walking to the other end of the roof where an elevated walkway connected to three other school buildings.

He turned a corner around a stone pillar and caught his breath for a second, massaging the bridge of his nose in thought.

He was probably going insane. Chasing Maya Halili down was not on his to-do list for today, and yet here he was, acting like a desperate fool.

He hadn't even thought of what he would say to her. He had a feeling she wouldn't take too kindly to him just walking up to her and apologizing.

I'm sorry for everything. I'm sorry I never apologized. I'm sorry that I've been secretly wiretapping you to extract information about the Seven Islands. I'm sorry that I've involved you in all of this. I'm sorry that I don't know what I'm doing. I'm sorry I've been so unkind to you. I'm sorry that I can't stop thinking about you. Do you want to get coffee with me?

He groaned. *What an idiot.* But what else was he supposed to do? He couldn't undo the past. He couldn't offer anything of value that would make up for it. All he had was time.

First-year Aga wouldn't have done anything. He would've stayed quiet, as he always was, and taken whatever people threw at him.

Maya wasn't like him. She caught what people threw at her and threw it right back, ten times harder.

Time would have to be enough. He would offer to make up for all the time they'd lost.

He had to think fast. He had to find her.

He readjusted his glasses and started walking.

Chapter 10

When Maya opened her eyes again, she was floating.

She realized that perhaps she had well and truly died, ferried off to the spirit realm by whichever god or deity was in charge of collecting the souls of the dead. She was lying down, moving back and forth like a piece of driftwood in the sea.

She wiggled her fingers one by one, then her toes, slowly feeling the rest of her body awaken with her. She opened her eyes, expecting to see the darkness of the Underworld and the face of the reaper. She blinked rapidly as the warmth of a yellow ceiling light shone in her eyes.

She sat up and looked around. The walls around her were a sickly white, with matching white drawers topped with boxes of face masks and bandages. She realized that she was on a clinic bed, right in the middle of a ward in the university clinic.

She wracked her brain for the reason why she was here.

Right. The pencil. Her *name.* Her *name* written on paper by an invisible hand.

She may not be dead, but she was, perhaps, having a mental breakdown.

She swung her legs to the side and stood up slowly, testing out her legs before walking out of the ward, looking around the hall for any signs of life.

She turned a corner and found herself in the infirmary lobby. The nurse on duty was clacking away on a typewriter. She was ancient, her messy grey hair the only thing Maya could see of her. She was hunched over the typewriter with her back to Maya, who let out a sigh of relief. *Not a spirit. A real person.*

'Hi,' she muttered quietly, unsure if there were any other people in the clinic. A quick glance at darkness outside the frosted front door told her that she had been in here for at least a few hours. 'I'm sorry to bother you, ma'am, but would you know how I got here?'

The nurse continued to type noisily, giving no signs that she had heard Maya speak. Maybe she was hard of hearing. She glanced up at the wall clock that read ten minutes until seven in the evening. Of course, the old lady wouldn't answer her. She probably thought Maya was still half dead.

'Ma'am,' Maya tried again, walking up to the front desk and leaning against the wood, 'thank you very much for taking care of me, but I'd really like to know how I ended up here.'

The noise of the typewriter filled the room. Save for her hands, the nurse's body was so eerily still.

'Okay . . .' Maya slowly backed up from the front desk, unsure of what to do. She looked around for a phone she could use or a form she could fill up and leave for the nurse to collect later, since she was very clearly busy at the moment.

'Anyway,' she said, 'I'm feeling much, much better now. If it's all right with you, I'll be heading back to my dorm room now.'

The front door jingled open, revealing dishevelled black hair and brown eyes framed by a pair of crocked glasses.

Aga Kaneko stepped into the university infirmary, his chest heaving slightly. His clothes were rumpled, his button down untucked on one side. His sleeves were pushed all the way up past his elbows, and the front of his shirt was drenched in sweat, revealing the smooth skin underneath.

Maya's body froze into place at the sight of him. For the first time since they met, Aga looked dishevelled and messy. His eyes had a wild look to them, like he had been looking for something. For someone.

'Halili,' he breathed. She stared back at him in silence.

'Kaneko.' His name caught in her throat. 'What the hell are you doing here?'

'You.' His voice was barely above a whisper. 'I was looking for you.'

Maya stared at him, unsure of what to say. 'Why?'

Aga's mouth opened, but no sound came out. His golden-brown eyes scanned her face until they landed on her lips. He sighed.

They stared at each other, the air crackling with energy, tendrils of uncertainty circling around them.

That was when they noticed the silence. The sounds of the typewriter had ceased. Maya looked back at the front desk.

The nurse had stood up without making a sound. Her back was still to them as she faced the wall, completely motionless.

Maya and Aga exchanged a look before the nurse spoke a single word.

'*Mayari*.'

Maya's blood turned cold.

'What did she just say?' Aga asked, his thick eyebrows knitting together.

'*Halili*,' the nurse said again, the last letter a sinister, hissing sound, the voice raking down Maya's spine like the pointed tip of a knife.

She felt a shadow move towards her right. Aga had stepped forward to stand beside her, his eyes locked on the nurse.

'Excuse me, ma'am.' He cleared his throat. 'Thank you very much for your help. I will escort Ms Halili to her dormitory. Good evening.'

Maya was just about to decline Aga's offer when the front door of the clinic opened once again.

A towering figure in a white doctor's coat entered the clinic. They were the tallest person Maya had ever seen in her life, their black ringlets cascading down their shoulders save for the small bun sitting atop their head. Each movement jostled the multiple piercings that adorned both their ears. Behind the curtain of curls, Maya could see a light-coloured birthmark in the centre of their forehead, its five points stretching outwards like a star.

The stranger smiled warmly at Maya, their sparkling white teeth framed by a shade of red.

'Hello, Maya.' Their melodic voice rang across the lobby. 'It's good to see you.'

Chapter 11

'I'm sorry, do I know you?'

'I'm happy to see that you're awake and well.' The doctor gestured to the exit door. 'I'm Maxim, the university physician on duty. I just got back from the main health services office to notify your family about what happened, so you're cleared to leave. I can escort you back to the dormitory to ensure that you're safe and sound.'

'That won't be necessary.' Aga stepped forward to block Maya from the physician's view. 'I can bring her home.'

Maya started to shake her head, taking a step back from the two of them. 'I'm already feeling well enough that I can manage it back home by myself.' She took another step towards the exit door, eyeing it to see if she could make it out of the clinic and away from this strange situation.

The physician took a step towards their left, blocking Maya's path to the exit door. 'Please, I insist.' They took a few steps towards the exit behind them, clicking it open but keeping hold of the handle. 'I just want to make sure you're in good health.'

Aga took another step forward, his large frame fully blocking Maya now. 'Thank you very much for your offer, Doc, but I can escort Ms Halili home.'

'Do you know this boy, Maya?' The physician eyed Aga suspiciously. 'You can never be too safe these days. Wouldn't want to report another missing student.' Their unwavering smile unsettled Maya. She could feel the hair on her arms rising in alarm.

Something is very, very wrong.

'I said I'm fine,' Maya said, stepping out from behind Aga. 'And I can go home by myself. Please let me through.'

A knock on the glass behind the physician rang through the emptiness of the clinic.

Maxim's eyebrows raised in confusion, turning around to open the door, revealing a foreign-looking bald man in a loose polo shirt and chino pants.

Aga groaned, the vibrations travelling down Maya's shoulder. He spoke in an angry, impatient tone towards the man in a language Maya had never heard of before. She could only assume it was Kiruvian.

The bald man responded, pushing through the clinic door and placing a large hand on Aga's shoulder, his response urgent.

'Maya.' Aga's worry was clear on his face, his eyes pleading. 'Let's go.'

'Maya.' Maxim's voice turned pleading, though their smile stayed on. 'Please let me escort you home. It's not safe.'

A croaking laugh sounded in the tight space of the clinic, sending a chill up Maya's spine.

Her eyes met with Maxim's, whose face slowly drained of colour. The bald man's eyes had focused on something behind them, his mouth dropping open. They turned towards the front desk.

The nurse was laughing. A deep, dark chuckle that shook her entire body. It felt like time had stopped as they watched in horror at the nurse, her laugh transforming into a frenzied cackle that got louder with every second that passed. Her whole body shook as she threw her head back to the ceiling, strands of spit glistening in between her rotten teeth.

In a split second, the nurse's tiny frame started cracking in all her joints, her limbs bending at unnatural angles, the terrifying laugh still coming out of her. The uniform on her back split open, revealing two giant, veiny wings. Her skin slowly turned a mottled grey, boils bubbling to the surface and coarse, black hair covering her arms. Her nails had grown into talons, curling in on themselves and touching the linoleum floor.

The creature that used to be the nurse grew taller, looming over them. It turned around to look at them, its eyes blood red and fixed on her.

'*Mayari Halili*,' it spoke, a booming and crackling sound that reverberated throughout the entire clinic. 'Your time has come.'

The demon smiled, revealing fangs and a row of sharp, rotting teeth.

Maxim turned towards the two of them with pure terror on their face. 'Run.'

Maya screamed as it launched itself across the front desk.

She felt herself being pulled down, her jaw hitting the floor hard. A warm, heavy body was on top of her, pinning her to the ground. She turned her face enough to see that Aga was on top of her, shielding her from the insane scene before them.

'Maya, don't look!' he yelled, his panicked breath hot on her ear.

Maya pushed herself up on her elbows and turned towards the centre of the clinic.

The bald man who had been standing beside them a few seconds ago had jumped in front of them to face the nurse-turned-monster. He pulled out a handgun and pointed it towards the creature. He turned towards them, pointing at the door.

Maxim was kneeling on the tiled floor, their arms held up to protect them. They had removed their white coat, revealing a long, flowing skirt in a vibrant purple hue and a sheer, billowing white blouse. Maya could see their back and arms completely tattooed with ancient-looking symbols.

'Out!' the bald man shouted in Kinadmani, a panicked look on his face.

The monster behind him let out an ear-piercing screech before it drove its talons through the bald man's skull.

Maya screamed.

A sickening, wet crunch filled the room as the creature crushed the remains of the man's head and pulled it off his body.

Maya closed her eyes as drops of blood spattered all over her face and hands.

'Tak,' she heard Maxim say. 'Okay, Mangaway. You've had your fun but take one step towards them and you'll find yourself right back in Kasanaan.'

Maya opened her eyes enough to see Maxim stand up and lift their hands up towards the monster, a bright white light emitting from their palms.

The monster that was Mangaway cackled, black liquid dripping down their pointy chin. 'You may try, babaylan.' The foul smell of burning flesh and sickness enveloped the room, choking Maya and stinging her eyes. 'But you will not banish me this time.' It grew even taller, the tips of its wings pressing against the ceiling and cracking the plaster. '*She* has granted me her power, and she will see to it that you are all dead by the end of the night.'

The monster rushed forward with a terrifying roar. Aga clasped his hand over her face, and for a moment she imagined Maxim would be split in half by the demon, their blood and guts splattered all over the floor.

Maya braced herself, but the impact never came. She opened her eyes.

A wall of bright white light stood before them, pulsing out of the physician's hands. She looked up just in time to see Mangaway jump through the light and completely disappear.

Maxim, still alive, looked down at them with their eyes glowing silvery white. 'Are you okay?'

Before Maya could respond, she heard Mangaway's shriek once again, this time from farther inside the clinic. Maya looked towards the back of the clinic lobby to see another wall of white light where Mangaway emerged, swinging its claws wildly in anger.

'What the tak is happening?' Aga yelled right above Maya's ear.

Mangaway ran towards them again, making the ground rumble beneath them. It jumped high into the air, fangs glistening against the white light.

It disappeared through the light again. Maya heard its screams echo through the clinic before she spotted the shadow of its wings behind the light on the other end of the room.

The walls weren't just made of light. They were *portals*.

The monster continued to attack, throwing its entire body weight at Maxim, who started moving their hands in twisting motions, moving the wall of light around as Mangaway's talons disappeared into it every time.

Maxim pushed the wall of light hard towards Mangaway, knocking it back several feet into a side wall before turning back to smile apologetically at them, their eyes still glowing. 'Should've listened to me when I told you to run.'

Mangaway stood up and doubled back towards them, clawing at Maxim's face with enough speed to push them back a step.

'Listen, I can't hold this thing forever, so here's the plan,' Maxim grunted as they continued to counter Mangaway's attacks. 'On the count of three, you are going to run out that door as fast as you can. I'll distract the old hag long enough for you to get a head start, then I'll find you. Lock all your doors and close all your windows. Turn off the lights and stand in the corner of your room farthest from any openings. If you hear a familiar voice calling you to come outside or a cry for help, do not answer. Do not open anything under any circumstances. Got it?' They faltered slightly as Mangaway's fangs snapped close towards the side of their face. Maya spotted blood trickling down their right earlobe.

She felt Aga's grip around her shoulders tightening in response. He was mumbling something under his breath, the same foreign language she couldn't understand, his breathing quick and laboured.

Mangaway's blood red eyes found hers. The demon flashed her a gruesome smile.

She had the sudden urge to vomit. She put a hand over her mouth, gagging at the sight and smell before her.

Maxim groaned. 'Please do not throw up on me. I'm going to count to three now. Ready?'

Mangaway drove another sharp talon towards them.

'You will die, babaylan!' it screeched. 'Bakunawa demands your blood!'

Maxim screamed, 'One, two, three!'

The wall of light disappeared as Maxim took a running leap towards Mangaway. They threw a ball of white light at the monster's face, causing it to throw its head back in pain. They used the momentum to get down on their knees and slide gracefully between Mangaway's legs, narrowly missing its grotesque belly. Maxim emerged on the other side, their glowing white eyes pulsing with power. 'Run!'

Maya jolted into motion, grabbing Aga's hand as she pushed through the exit door and pulled him as hard as she could and ran.

'Come on, demon! Show me what you've got!'

She looked over her shoulder in time to see Maxim walking slowly backwards, a taunting smile on their face as they led Mangaway further into the clinic.

The clinic door swung shut as the lights turned off, surrounding them both in darkness.

Chapter 12

Aga uttered a silent prayer to his gods that he had enough stamina to keep up with Maya.

His breaths came out in puffs of cold air as he and Maya sprinted across the university. The night was cold and the moon was high in the sky, and he prayed that there was enough moonlight to see ahead of him.

Despite his obvious height advantage, Maya was a much faster runner. They ran for what felt like hours, their thighs burning and their lungs heaving. The university was eerily quiet around them, save for their feet hitting the pavement.

Aga had a sinking feeling that the quiet was not a good sign.

He had no idea where they were going, only that Maya was ahead of him and leading them away from the infirmary. They ran all the way to the lesser-known back road that led outside the campus. They turned a few corners, splashing into puddles on their way, before turning on to a small cul-de-sac with a circle of short apartment buildings.

They stopped in front of a faded orange building, shivering and drenched in sweat. Aga's dress shirt was stuck to the skin on his back and his lungs felt like they were on fire. He stole a quick glance at Maya, her hair all frizzy and her tan skin glistening with sweat under the moonlight. He felt the sudden impulse to pull her close and breathe all of her in.

He shook his head free of the thought. His mind must still be reeling from what he just saw.

A stranger with glowing eyes that could manipulate the light around them like a weapon. A winged demon disguised as a nurse. *He was going insane.*

'They knew my name.'

Aga straightened at the sound of Maya's voice. She was bent over, her hand clutching her heart. 'They knew my *name*, Kaneko,' she hissed.

'What name?' he asked. 'Mayari?'

She hesitated. 'Yes,' she replied. 'My real name.'

Mayari. The Old World goddess of the moon.

'Yes, so we've gathered. How is that possible?' A disbelieved laugh escaped him. 'How is anything we've just seen even remotely possible?'

'I don't know,' she breathed. 'I don't know.'

He tilted his face up towards the moon as he tried to sort through the mess of his thoughts. This entire day would shave a few years off his life. There would be no coming back from this. Especially not with his father.

'Why did you come?'

He turned back to look at her. She was standing tall now, finally recovered from their sprint. Her eyes were blazing with an intensity that dared him to look away.

He found that he couldn't, not when she was looking at him like that.

Tell her, his inner voice urged. *Wipe the slate clean.*

'I don't know,' he said quietly.

She was silent for a heartbeat. Perhaps she knew better than he did. *Please, gods, let her understand what I do not have the words to explain.*

'But how did you find me?' She took a step closer. 'Better yet, how did you know where to find me?'

He paused. He didn't actually know. He had run all over campus looking for her, unsure of where to go. But just at just the right moment, he felt an invisible force pulling him and guiding him along, pushing him towards the infirmary.

He couldn't exactly tell her that.

'Maya, I . . .'

His words were cut off by Maya's piercing shriek as she was tackled by a pale, lanky body.

Aga barely had a moment to react before the body wrapped its arms around her and squeezed. He yelped and moved to yank Maya away until he realized that she was hugging the body back.

'What the tak?' the body spoke. 'What are you doing here?'

It took a step backward, allowing the moonlight to illuminate the face attached to it.

Hanan Halili stood before them, barefoot in a ratty green shirt and jean shorts. 'I found you unconscious on the floor of our room! I thought you had a stroke! What happened to you?' She shook Maya gently, speaking in what Aga recognized as Hiwagani.

Aga had heard of Maya's younger sister. It was impossible not to, not when every student at NUSI was pining for her attention. She was undoubtedly beautiful, Aga thought. But his eyes strayed back to Maya, who looked like she was about to cry.

Hanan continued, giving Maya a once-over and smoothing a hand over her hair. 'I wanted to stay with you, but the nurse said I had to leave. I would've stayed all night if I could.'

At this, Maya burst into tears, falling into Hanan's arms and holding her tight. 'Oh, Han,' she said in between sobs. 'Something terrible just happened.'

'What are you talking about? Did something bad happen to you at the infirmary?' Hanan's voice turned cold. 'And why is the Kaneko guy here? Did he hurt you?'

Aga felt a warmth momentarily bloom in his chest. *Has Maya been talking about me with her sister?* Only for him to be slightly offended at the realization that she didn't know his first name.

'Um,' he cleared his throat, 'I assure you that I did nothing of the sort.'

Maya sniffled, putting a calming hand on Hanan. 'Let's go inside. It's not safe out here.' She pulled on her sister's arm urgently. Hanan's protective stance softened at Maya's touch as she turned around and started walking back into the dormitory lobby. Aga stood there, unsure if he was supposed to follow.

'Come on, Kaneko,' Maya called out to him. 'We can talk in the study room.'

He ran after them.

Chapter 13

Maya all but pushed Hanan and Aga into the empty study room before locking the door behind her. She turned to the windows on the opposite side of the room and closed each one, pulling the curtains and flicking off the lights, plunging them into complete darkness.

'Okay . . .' Hanan's voice was hesitant. 'Okay, this is fine. Mind explaining why we need to talk in complete darkness?' she said in Hiwagani.

'In Kinadmani, Han,' Maya whispered. 'Kaneko can't understand.'

'Actually,' Aga spoke, his Hiwagani soft and calm, 'I can. Understand, I mean.' Maya could practically see him shrugging his shoulders. 'Linguistics major.'

Only Aga Kaneko could make Maya roll her eyes at a time like this.

'Hanan, listen to me,' she spoke into the darkness. 'I am going to sound insane and you're not going to believe me, but I need you to at least pretend that you do for the time being, because I don't even know if *I* believe in myself. Okay?' Maya let out a shaky breath.

She felt Hanan take a step towards her before clasping their hands together. 'I don't even need to know what you're about to say to know that I already believe you. Just tell me.'

Maya took a deep breath before she did just that. She recounted her experience in their dorm room with the invisible force that had taken control of her body, forcing her to write down the cryptic message on her notebook. She described waking up in the infirmary to Aga, a terrifying nurse that turned out not to be a nurse, and the strange physician with glowing eyes that saved their lives. By the end of it, she was crying again, silent tears streaming down her face as she tried her best to breathe in between her hiccups.

Hanan held her hands the entire time, listening attentively and rubbing comforting circles into her palms. 'Han, I don't know what to do.'

She felt Hanan let out a long sigh. 'I have something to tell you, too.'

Maya could feel her stomach drop. 'What's wrong?'

Hanan squeezed Maya's hands tighter. 'Earlier today, during my date with Anton Ortiguera. It didn't go well.'

'Oh, Han,' Maya said. 'I'm sorry.'

'Wait, I'm not done. We . . .' Hanan swallowed thickly. 'I said something stupid, something I shouldn't have said in public. A couple of Astyrian soldiers overheard me.'

Maya's grip on her sister's hands tightened. 'What did they do?'

'That's not the important part.' Hanan shook her head impatiently. 'One of them tried to scare me, but right before he could actually do something, a blast of water came out of nowhere and completely soaked them both.' Hanan's eyes took on a faraway look on her face. 'And there was a boy. He pulled me away from it.' She pointed at her forehead. 'His eyes were glowing and there was a star-shaped mark right above his eyebrows. Just like that doctor.'

Maya thought about the similar scar on Maxim's forehead. 'What did he want?'

'Nothing. He just stared at me.' She lifted her hands, wiggling her fingers around in the air. 'But there were droplets of water suspended in the air around him. He waved his hand, and they started dancing and twisting into strange shapes. It was unlike anything I've ever seen. I thought for sure that I was hallucinating.'

A doctor who can open portals. A boy who can make water dance. It was all too similar and convenient for it to be merely a coincidence.

'What do we do?' Hanan said, her voice a trembling whisper.

Maya was silent. *I wish I knew.*

Behind them, Aga cleared his throat. 'The physician called the monster in the clinic by its name. *Mangaway.*' He paused. 'Does that name sound familiar to you?'

'Mangaway,' Hanan spoke the name slowly, fear tainting her voice. 'The spirit of disease?' She turned to face Maya with wide, searching eyes.

'Nanay,' Maya choked out. 'Nanay used to tell us stories. She used to tell us all about the spirits and gods of the Old World.'

She remembered her mother's story about Mangaway. The old hag brought disease and bad luck to households, siphoning away the life and energy of unsuspecting souls. In her favourite story, Mangaway was defeated by the warrior Haliya, who sent it back to Kasanaan, the spirit realm.

A cold wind blew past them, ruffling Maya's hair. She welcomed the cool breeze, until she remembered.

The doors and windows are supposed to be locked.

A soft rustling came from the corner of the room near the windows.

'Do you guys hear that?' Aga said.

Maya could feel Hanan's breath quicken with panic. She heard Aga take a step towards them, his hand brushing against her forearm before gently resting on her skin.

'Maya?' Hanan whispered.

Maya had barely survived an attempt on her life, but she could not let whatever was in the room with them lay a hand on Hanan.

She lunged for the light switch on the back wall, flicking it on and jumping away to the corner. She spotted a pencil on her study desk and picked it up, holding it up before her like a sword.

Maxim sat crouching on the floor of the study room, curly black hair dishevelled and falling out of the bun on their head, the front of their white blouse soaked in blood. They were breathing hard with a hand on their chest. They looked up at Maya holding the pencil. 'I admire your bravery, but you might want to sharpen that next time.'

Maya looked down at the unsharpened pencil for a split second before throwing it at Maxim with a yell.

It bounced harmlessly off their shoulder, earning her an eye roll from them. 'I guess I deserved that.'

They stood up from their spot on the floor, dusting off their skirt which now had whole chunks of fabric missing from it, revealing their cut-up calves and knees.

'How did you get in here?' Maya demanded, moving sideways towards Hanan who was standing in shocked silence in the middle of the room. 'Who are you and what do you want from me?' Maxim took a step towards them, making Maya take a step back. 'Take one more step and I'll scream.'

Maxim put their hands up in surrender. 'Relax, I'm not gonna kill you. If I wanted to, I would've done it by now.' They stretched a hand towards Maya. 'Maxim Aganad, babaylan. I've been waiting a long time for you, Mayari.'

Maya blinked in disbelief, staring at their outstretched hand. 'I thought you were a doctor.'

'Well, I am. But that's not important.' Maxim took back their hand and looked at Hanan, just now realizing she was in the room with them. They pointed suspiciously at her. 'Do you know her? I don't think she should be in here with us while we're discussing sensitive information.'

'Hanan isn't going anywhere.' Maya crossed her arms. 'Either she stays, or you go.'

'Oh!' Maxim clapped their hands together. 'You're Hanan! Marikit's youngest daughter.' They made a kissing face at her. 'So lovely to finally meet you.'

That startled Maya out of her shock. 'How do you know our mother?' she demanded. '*Who are you?*'

'Fine.' Maxim rolled their eyes, blowing out a breath. 'Let's do this slowly, then.' They pointed at themselves. '*Babaylan.*' They enunciated every syllable. 'Sound familiar?'

'Shaman,' Aga spoke up. 'It means shaman, right?'

'Ha! Someone's been paying attention.' Maxim clapped again.

'That's impossible,' Hanan piped in. 'The babaylan don't exist any more. The practise of the Old World religion was outlawed centuries ago. Those rituals don't work.'

Maxim's eyes twinkled with mischief. 'What if I told you that the Old World religion was outlawed but not forgotten?' Their eyes emitted a faint white glow. 'What if I told you that the babaylan are very much real, and that we've been hiding in plain sight since the Marinese first came to our shores?' They smiled.

'We?' Maya exclaimed. 'There's more of you?' That would explain the mysterious man that Hanan encountered in the alleyway.

'Oh, yes. You'll meet the others eventually.' Maxim waved a dismissive hand at her before looking pointedly at Hanan. 'Sorry about Alon, by the way. He's still fairly new at this, and he's not big on using his words. He thought you were Maya.' They pointed at Hanan and smiled apologetically. 'Happens to the best of us.'

Maya's mind was racing. It felt like her entire life was being upended in front of her. *How is any of this possible?*

'Anyway, as I was saying,' Maxim cleared their throat, 'we've been waiting for you for a long time. I for one am grateful to the spirits for finally reaching you, because they could not have picked a better time.'

'Why?' Maya asked warily. 'What's happening?' She pointed at herself. 'And why have you been waiting for *me*?'

Their eyes flashed with another pulse of white glow. 'Are you familiar with the story of Bakunawa?'

Maya froze. Another demon from her mother's stories. The ancient sea serpent of greed and hunger, the harbinger of destruction and chaos, the demon Bakunawa. *She who devours.*

Maxim nodded knowingly. 'I can see Marikit prepared you well. Bakunawa, the oldest known demon of the Old World, is awake.'

'What?' Maya shrieked. 'What do you mean, awake?'

'She's back,' Maxim said grimly. 'Once every few hundred years, demons from Kasanaan manifest back into the real world. It is the way of the universe according to the Old World. That's why the babaylan have been around for just as long.' They spread their arms wide, exposing their tattooed chest and arms. 'We are the last remaining line of defence of the Old World and its magic.' They let out a heavy sigh. 'But Bakunawa is different. She is very, very old. She hasn't manifested out of Kasanaan in thousands of years. The last known account of a babaylan defeating Bakunawa was—'

'Kaylahon,' Maya interrupted. 'Babaylan Kaylahon.'

Maxim nodded. 'Exactly.'

'I'm sorry,' Maya held her hands up, 'but what does this have to do with me? And you still haven't answered my first question. How do you know my mother?'

Maxim gave her a soft smile. 'Your mother would be so proud.'

Maya groaned. 'What does that even mean?'

Maxim met her gaze. 'Marikit was one of us, Maya. She was a babaylan.'

In that instant, it felt like the floor was pulled from underneath Maya. Her mother. A babaylan.

'That's impossible.' Maya faltered, flicking through her memories of her mother in her mind. 'Nanay was the village captain.' Back in Hiwaga, fifteen years ago. A simple, normal life in a bamboo house by the sea. Marikit had been an anchor in their community, and a beacon of light in their home. Marikit was their everything.

Right before she was taken from them.

'That's not right. Nanay was taken by the Astyrians.' Her chest felt tight as the words left her. 'We never saw her again after that.' She swallowed hard. 'If she was really a babaylan, why didn't she defend herself?'

Her mother had been missing for so long that she had been presumed dead. No one had ever found anything to prove otherwise.

'Marikit Halili, you are under arrest for insubordination against the Astyrian military.' The Astyrian soldier pulled their mother hard by the shoulder, pushing her to the ground. Marikit's face landed in the dirt, and the Astyrian soldier pressed a steel-toed boot in between her shoulder blades.

'Nanay!' Maya screamed, carrying an infant Hanan in her arms. She stood behind her father, who was clutching their grandmother to his chest, restraining her as she wailed.

'Please, stop it!' Marikit exclaimed, spitting dirt out of her bloody mouth. 'I'll cooperate. Just don't hurt my children.'

'Marikit, wait!' Danilo yelled desperately. He pushed their grandmother aside, taking a step towards the soldiers. Every single one of them held up their handguns.

Their father pressed his forehead against one of their barrels. 'Go ahead, shoot me! Take my life in exchange for hers!' he screamed at them. The Astyrians hesitated.

'Go on, you cowards! Do it!'

'Danilo, no!' Marikit screamed at him. 'The girls! Think of the girls!' She wept as she continued to beg him. 'Please, Danilo. Take them inside. Please,' she pleaded with him. 'Take care of the girls. Promise me,' she screamed. 'Promise me!'

At that, their father hesitated. Tears ran down his cheeks as regarded his wife lying face down in the soil. Slowly, he lifted his head away from the gun pointed at him.

The Astyrian soldiers laughed. 'That's right. Listen to your traitorous village captain of a wife.' The one stepping on their mother's back pressed her harder into the ground. 'Maybe that'll make you think twice about disobeying Astyrian orders next time.' He pulled her up by her hair, shaking her hard. 'I know it was you who set fire to our base. Now you get to watch while we burn down every home on this side of Hiwaga.'

Maya felt her cheeks dampen. She was crying.

Maxim's smile fell. 'Maya, I'm so sorry. We know what happened to your mother. That's why we're here.' They pushed the curls off their forehead. 'Your mother was the bravest babaylan I had ever met. She cared more about her family than herself. When I was first called by the spirits, it was your mother who found me, took care of me, and trained me. When she decided to go off on her own to start a family, I was excited for her. She was carving out her own path and deciding her fate on her own, despite the responsibility that the spirits had given her.' Maxim's eyes glistened under the dim study room light. 'When I heard of what happened, I was devastated. She was like an older sister to me.' They looked down at the ground. 'It felt like the spirits were punishing her from running away from her destiny.'

'What destiny?' Maya asked.

Maxim took a deep breath. 'Your mother wasn't just any babaylan. She was the descendant of Kaylahon.' They pointed at the five-pointed star above their eyebrows. 'All babaylan are direct descendants of the most loyal followers of Kaylahon, the first babaylan. There were five of them in total, and each one dedicated their lives to learning Kaylahon's way of life. When Kaylahon passed, her power passed on to her next living descendant of age, and they formed a group strong enough to defend the Old World from the spirits and demons that threatened to destroy it. That was how the Hand of Kaylahon was born.' They pointed at her. 'And you, my dear girl, are the next living descendant of your mother. *You* are the spirit of Kaylahon.'

The pit in Maya's stomach grew. This couldn't be happening.

'That's why the spirits are calling to you. You're of age, and the universe is demanding that you take your place.'

'Is that why I've been seeing them everywhere?' Maya whispered. 'Is that . . . is that why they wrote down my name in my notebook?'

Maxim nodded. 'The Hand was getting by these past fifteen years, but right now, we *need* you. Something bad is happening in the Seven Islands, Maya. Don't tell me you haven't noticed.'

Maya thought about the missing people all over Santa Teresita. 'I've noticed. Do you have anything to do with that?'

Maxim scoffed. 'Gods, no. But there was a reason Mangaway tried to attack you today. Demons who haven't been spotted for hundreds of years have been manifesting back into our world. We're talking about hundreds of them, all over the Islands. And they're going after the few who have any hope of stopping them, like you and me.'

'But why?' Maya countered. 'What do they want?'

'We don't know yet. We think it could be connected to Bakunawa waking up. All we do know is that *she* is back.' Maxim shuddered.

'How do you know?' Hanan squeaked. 'How do you know she's real?'

'Back in the clinic, Mangaway said her name,' Maya said slowly. 'It said that Bakunawa demands our blood.' Her eyes met Maxim's. 'Could Bakunawa be sending all these demons up to our world?'

The room was silent for a second before Aga let out a frustrated yelp.

'Oh, this is ridiculous!' Aga threw his hands up in the air. 'None of this can possibly be real. I've never even heard of the babaylan outside of textbooks. How do we know you're not just making this up?'

'Do you know this man?' Maxim pointed an accusing finger at Aga. 'Is this the same guy who was bothering you at the infirmary? I can get rid of him for you, if you want.' Their eyes started glowing white again.

'No!' Maya jumped in front of Aga, her hands out in front of her like a shield. 'He's not bothering me. He helped me back at the infirmary.' She hesitated. 'He's not Islander. He doesn't know what he's talking about.' She looked back at Aga apologetically.

Aga seemed to have the sense not to defend himself. He stayed quiet, his eyes trained down at the floor.

'Why did Mangaway say that?' she spoke to Maxim. 'Why would Bakunawa need our blood?'

For once, Maxim looked unsure. 'We don't know. Bakunawa is one of the oldest demons in existence. Most of what we know about her died out with the older generations of babaylan.'

'How do we stop her?' Maya demanded. 'What do we do?'

'I can show you.' Maxim lifted a hand up, and a glowing orb appeared in their palm.

Maya rubbed her eyes with the palms of her hands. 'Okay, sure. I feel like I'm going insane. But okay.'

Maxim's eyes shone with an unreadable emotion. 'I can explain everything in time.' They reached out a hand for Maya to take. 'But you have to know that we're here because of your mother. We promised her that we would come for you when it was your time. And I intend to make good on that promise.'

'Why didn't she tell us?' Hanan asked angrily. 'And why is all of this responsibility on Maya? I was her daughter, too.'

'It's complicated.' Maxim looked at Hanan. 'All you have to know is that it's not you they're looking for.'

Hanan pressed her lips together and turned away.

'I can tell you everything you want to know about your mother, your bloodline, and your destiny. I can open your eyes to the spirit realm and the underworld. I will teach you how to call down the gods and spirits. I will train you to turn your body into their vessel. I will show you how to defend yourself against any spirit or demon you come across. You will take your place in the Hand of Kaylahon.' Maxim gave Maya's shoulder a squeeze. 'But only when you're ready.'

They took a step back, much to Maya's surprise. 'The spirits can only call to you. To answer them is your choice.'

'And what happens if I decide not to?' she challenged.

'Then they'll keep bothering you until you do. The spirits don't really know how to take no for an answer.' Maxim shrugged. 'Listen, I know this is a lot, and I for one am not in the practise of forcing people into situations they aren't prepared for.' Maxim turned away, stretching their arms over their head like a cat. 'Really sorry to be dumping all of this on you now, circumstances and all that. I'll be going now.'

'Wait, what?' Maya reached for Maxim, thinking to touch their arm but deciding not to after seeing it was also drenched in blood. 'Where are you going? You can't just leave me here! What if that demon comes back?' Maya shuddered at the thought. Hanan and Aga remained by her side, both stony-faced and silent.

'Don't worry about Mangaway. I sent that diseased hag back to the spirit realm, so it won't be bothering us for another hundred years, probably. And I'm not leaving for good.' They looked around the study room suspiciously. 'Just think about what I said and let it sink in. I'll come back for you tomorrow.'

They reached into their skirt pocket and pulled out an amber-coloured vial with a thick yellow liquid inside that was swirling around by itself, the droplets glowing and in constant motion.

'I think it's safe to open your doors and windows now. I can't guarantee something else isn't going to attack you while I'm gone, so just in case, take this.'

Maxim tossed it towards Maya, who caught it with both her hands, cupping it tenderly like an egg. 'What is this?' The amulet was warm to the touch, thrumming with power.

'If you ever come face to face with another demon or malevolent spirit, break that amulet on the ground. I'll be alerted that you're in danger, and it'll offer you temporary protection while you wait for me to reach you.' Maxim gestured for Maya to place it around her neck.

Maya lifted the amulet over her head and let it sit in the middle of her chest. It glowed even brighter when it came into contact with her skin.

'We'll be waiting. Try not to get killed before then.' Maxim threw a wink at the two girls and a dumbstruck Aga before pressing their palms together, a warm light flooding the entire room.

The three of them shielded their eyes for a moment, only to find that the strange physician had vanished, leaving behind droplets of blood on the tiled floor.

Chapter 14

Aga was going to be sick.

His stomach was churning, his head was throbbing, and he couldn't help but slump in his seat at the very back of the lecture hall. His seatmate was a first-year girl who had been side-eyeing him since class started. She didn't know that he had to squeeze his eyes shut every couple of minutes just to keep his insides intact. Aga didn't care. He didn't even remember her name.

Dr Tolentino was up front, shuffling back and forth in front of the blackboard as he spoke in rapid-fire Kinadmani about pre-colonial Island life. The professor had very abruptly asked Aga to sit in as his teaching assistant for his morning class, and Aga didn't have it in him to say no. That was how he landed himself in the back of a freshman classroom at three in the afternoon.

'The pre-colonial Islanders believed Bathala to be the almighty god and creator.' Dr. Tolentino pressed his hands together in a prayer position. 'And legend said that those who revered him the most would be granted the gift of immortality and magical powers.'

The events of last night replayed themselves in Aga's memory. Maxim had completely uprooted his entire understanding of reality. He wouldn't have believed any of it to be true, maybe would have even chalked it up to some nasty insomnia-induced hallucination.

Except there was proof, and it was sitting around Maya's neck.

'People tried their best, of course, but there is no evidence to prove that any of them became magical.' This earned a few chuckles from the class. 'Or that the folk tales of their time were based on fact. Take for example the village of Banwa.' He raised a shaky, chalk-covered hand to the board and drew a crude drawing of a house. 'We have no evidence to prove that such a place existed, and yet the tales surrounding Bakunawa, the moon-eating serpent, were all based here.' He then proceeded to draw seven circles on the board.

That immediately caught Aga's attention. He sat up straighter, eager to listen to his professor.

After Maxim had mysteriously vanished, the three of them had stood in the study room in complete silence for a good couple of minutes. Hanan was the first one to break the silence.

'Well,' she said, 'I definitely believe you now.'

'Are you sure?' Maya replied, her voice bleak. 'I still don't believe me. I think I need to sit down.'

'I believe you,' Aga said quietly as he shoved his hands into his pockets and looked down at his shoes. 'You're not crazy.'

'But this entire situation is.'

They didn't have much to say after that, other than agreeing that they all needed to sort through their thoughts and sleep on them. Maya and Hanan promised that they would reach out to Aga if they saw anything or, the gods forbid, something happened to one of them, and Aga did the same.

He had chosen not to call his father when he got home. He didn't need to know about any of this.

Dr Tolentino continued to talk. 'In the old folk tales, Bakunawa was a ravenous spirit who thought the seven moons were the most delicious-looking things she had ever laid eyes on.' More laughter erupted from around the classroom. 'And so, she flew out of the sea like a great beast, destroying everything in her path. She flew into the sky and ate each moon, one by one.' He pointed at the seven circles on the board. 'The village shaman, Babaylan Kaylahon, saw Bakunawa rise from the ocean and tried to warn the rest of Banwa, but they chose not to believe her.' He proceeded to erase six of the seven moons. 'Until there was only one left.'

It was that word again. *Babaylan.*

'Bathala saw the destruction that Bakunawa had caused from his castle in the sky and wept. He heard Babaylan Kaylahon calling him, asking for his help. To save his people, he sent the gods and spirits down to share their powers with Kaylahon. They inhabited Kaylahon's body, who then used their gifts to protect the remaining seventh moon.'

Dr Tolentino drew the silhouette of a woman on the board and shaded it in with his chalk. 'Kaylahon allowed the gods to use her body as a vessel to defeat Bakunawa.

Together, they plunged the magical bolo knife K'filan into Bakunawa's side, sending her to the depths of Kasanaan for eternity.'

It was at that exact moment the bell in between periods rang. The ringing jolted Aga out of his trance, and he blinked once, twice before grounding himself back in reality.

'My apologies, it seems that I let myself get carried away with storytelling again.' He clapped his wrinkled hands together. 'We'll continue with the evolution of the Kinadmani language next session.'

The sound of screeching chairs on wood floors resounded throughout the lecture hall as students made their ways to their next classes.

Aga stood up quickly, allowing all the freshmen students to exit the back door first while he gathered up his things.

'Aga.'

He looked up at the melodic sound of his name and came face to face with Maya.

She stood before him, one step lower on the staircase, her face tilted upwards towards him, her eyes shining like stars. For a second, his heartbeat quickened. Was she here to see him?

Then he remembered. *Idiot.* Maya had a lecture in the same classroom right after Dr Tolentino.

'Hi' was all he could come up with.

She gave him a small smile. 'Hi.'

He let out a long breath. 'How are you?'

She laughed under her breath, a small one that made his heart sing. 'We almost died last night, and you wanna know how I am?'

'Well, yes.' He took a step down the stairs, moving to the side to face her. They were level now, but she had to tilt her head back to look at him.

'I mean.' His brain stuttered for a moment. She was so close that he could smell her perfume, the same scent she wore on the night they were attacked in the infirmary. *Rose and jasmine.* 'After everything that happened last night, I'd want to know.'

Maya sighed. 'I don't know.' She looked down at her feet. 'I really don't know.'

Aga looked down at his feet. Affirming words weren't his strongest suit. 'It's all right not to know yet. Maxim did say that they'd give you some time to let it sink in.' He took a step back up the stairs with every intention of leaving it at that, until he turned around and saw the dark look on Maya's face. He knew that look a little too well.

It was fear. Fear and confusion about things that had just been revealed but made no sense.

The words came out of him before he had time to think them through. 'There's this coffee stall right beside Jorge Hall that I always pass by when I'm working late nights.' It was his turn to give her a small smile. 'It's not exactly night-time yet, but it always makes me feel better. They have great barako.'

Maya's eyes brightened at the mention of coffee. 'I think I know that place. I've never tried anything from them, though.' She plunged her hand into her canvas bag. 'But barako sounds good. And I need to pass by later anyway. Need to submit something to Dr Manalo.'

'Perfect.' Aga's smile was wider now. 'See you later.'

Chapter 15

'I take it back.'

A few hours later, Maya hesitated before she took another sip of her coffee, the bitter liquid sloshing inside her paper cup as she tipped it towards her mouth. It coated her tongue, making her wince and stick her tongue out in disgust. She let out a cough as she forcibly gulped it down her throat. 'Do you drink this every day?' Did she really rush all the way here after her last lecture for this?

'Not every day.' Aga's eyes twinkled with mischief from behind his cup. 'Just on the days I need to forget I'm human.'

'Clearly.' Maya forced herself to take another tiny sip out of courtesy before placing the half-empty cup beside her on the bench. She wasn't about to throw away a free cup of coffee. 'I'm sorry, I lied about wanting barako.' She smiled apologetically at Aga. 'I don't actually drink coffee.'

Aga put his cup down to look squarely at her. 'Why?'

Maya shrugged. 'It messes with my nerves. I'm already forgetful and disorganized as it is. Coffee doesn't help.'

Aga shook his head. 'I mean, why did you lie about wanting barako?'

Maya was quiet for a moment. 'Because it seemed like something you enjoyed, and I didn't want to say no.'

Aga stared at her, a red flush creeping up his neck. 'Okay. I appreciate it.' He ducked his head and smiled. 'But you don't need to lie about wanting to do things if you don't want to, Maya. I'd rather you tell me the truth about not liking something than try to please me.'

Maya stared at him, completely dumbfounded. This was the same Aga Kaneko who she traded barbed words with, the same Aga Kaneko who had tormented for the past five years. And he was being nice to her. The world was turning upside down.

She cleared her throat. 'Okay, then. I'll be honest. Only demons would consider this as sustenance. You know you can add stuff in it, right? Normal human things like milk and sugar?' She turned to Aga, who choked on his barako.

He took a fist to his chest, beating at it to stop the choking and laughed. 'Unlike you, I have taste.' He tipped his cup all the way back before crumpling it in his hand, the contents completely drained. The frontmost strands of his black hair fell on his forehead and touched his eyelashes. Maya had the sudden overwhelming desire to push them back from his forehead to see his face better.

What? She shook her head free from the thought before she could fully examine it. She had the feeling she ought to examine what the past twenty-four hours meant for her first.

She still wouldn't have believed the entire thing to be true, except she had proof of it around her neck, vibrating softly and sitting comfortably on her chest. She didn't know what to make of it, and she wasn't anywhere near making a choice, but in the back of her mind, a small voice was whispering to consider it.

Babaylan. Even thinking it sounded ridiculous to Maya. There was a part of her that felt excited for the first time in a long while.

She was a babaylan. A descendant of Kaylahon, one of the most powerful beings to ever live. A pillar of the Old World and its former magic.

But an overwhelming sense of dread was consuming her. Never mind the fact that she already had a million things going on in her life that she was struggling to balance. If she said yes to the spirits, would she get the answers she wanted? Would she finally understand her past and her mother?

Could she learn how to be a babaylan in time to stop Bakunawa?

And if she answered the call of the spirits and failed to do what she was supposed to, what then? Who would suffer because of her?

'You know,' Aga interrupted Maya's thoughts, 'Dr Tolentino always says to me that he can hear my thoughts all the way from where he's seated.' He tapped his temple with a finger. 'I think I get it now. Your thoughts are written all over your face.'

'Sorry.' She sighed, imagining that all her jumbled-up thoughts and emotions were leaving her body. 'It's just a lot.'

'I can't imagine what it must be like,' Aga said. 'Having all of that information dumped on you in one night. About the missing students and your mother. I'm sorry.'

'Yeah.' Maya thought back to a bedtime story her mother had told her as a child. The memory played itself back for her.

'We are all born with a little magic within us,' Marikit spoke soothingly, running her gentle hands through Maya's wild curls while she sat in her lap, 'but some are chosen by the gods to hold more magic within them than others.' She smiled down at Maya. 'Like Babaylan Kaylahon.'

Young Maya clapped in delight. 'That's my favourite story! Babaylan Kaylahon was so brave. I want to be like her.' She jumped down from her mother's lap and zoomed around the room, pretending to be a legendary warrior-shaman from the tales of old.

Marikit shook her head amusedly at the sight of her tireless daughter. 'I know you will be, little star. You may not know it yet, but you are so very special.' Maya giggled, crawling in between her mother's legs as she sat at the windowsill. 'Remember this when you look up at the sky,' Marikit said as she picked Maya up and placed her back on her lap, angling her towards the open window. 'The gods look down upon you with love. You are blessed beyond measure, and you will own the sky and the stars one day if you are willing to accept them.'

Aga stood up, jostling the bench beneath Maya. She looked up at him, and for the first time noticed the light freckles spattering his nose.

'We can pass by Jorge Hall now, if you like.' He shoved his hands into his pockets, fishing out a ring of keys and smiling down at her. 'I need to pass by Dr Tolentino's office, too. Accidentally forgot to return the keys to his drop box.' He held out his hand to her.

Maya eyed Aga's outstretched hand. She took it, albeit cautiously, before he pulled her up from the bench. Before she knew it, she was losing her balance, colliding with Aga, their chests bumping and his barako splashing onto the pavement.

'Oh gods, I'm sorry!' she immediately exclaimed, wrapping her hand around the cup in Aga's hand to steady it. 'You lost half your cup because of me.'

Aga stood motionless as he stared down at her, cheeks flushed and lips parted. Maya realized a moment too late that her hand was wrapped tightly around Aga's instead of the cup. Without thinking, she squeezed his hand, feeling the soft skin give way.

Aga gasped, a hand coming up to Maya's shoulder. 'Maya,' he sputtered, 'we should go.' He gently pushed her away, transferring his cup to the other hand and flexing the one that Maya held.

Her cheeks heated in embarrassment. What was she thinking? Why on earth did she have to do that? And to *Aga Kaneko* of all people? He probably thought she was trying to flirt with him!

'Come on,' she said as she walked past him and up the steps of Jorge Hall. She tried her best to mask her red cheeks along the way.

The front desk was empty for the first time when they entered the centre. It didn't seem like Mrs Abad was on duty tonight, much to Maya's relief. In fact, it didn't seem like anyone was at the office tonight. Perhaps there was a faculty-wide event.

'I'll be quick,' she called over her shoulder to Aga as she made her way down the hallway towards Dr Manalo's office. 'Meet you back here in a bit.'

Aga waved her off. 'Don't worry about it. I'll go check if Dr Tolentino's in.'

She knocked gently on the door before calling out to her professor. 'Dr Manalo? It's Maya Halili.' The inside of the office was silent. Maya thought about knocking again, raising her first to the door a second time before it opened suddenly, revealing Dr Manalo in a grey pantsuit, her long black hair around her shoulders, her green glasses popping against her dark red lipstick. She couldn't help but stare at her professor's dazzling smile.

'Oh, hello, Maya.' She opened the door wider, revealing her office cloaked in darkness. 'I wasn't expecting you today. Please, come in.' Dr Manalo flicked on the lights, flooding her office in a warm yellow light, casting shadows shaped like books and trinkets across the walls.

'Thank you so much for making time for me again.' Maya stepped into the office, breathing in the familiar smell of sea salt from the candle on the desk. She took a seat across from Dr Manalo, who was lounging casually in her leather chair, her chin resting on her interlaced fingers.

Maya pulled out a few sheets of paper from her satchel. 'I actually wanted to show you some updated research I did on your new project on Islandic mythology.' She brought out a folder from her satchel, a sheath of typewritten words that she had finished in the school library. 'I thought it would be interesting to include some legends about other lesser-known spirits.'

Dr Manalo took the papers in her hands, looking over her glasses at the words. 'I have to say Maya, you continue to exceed my expectations.' She chuckled, tapping the bottom of the stack back into alignment. 'Now, enough about work.' She leaned forward on her desk. 'How are you, my dear? Forgive me, but I have to ask, since you've been working on my research for me for the past six months. Are you doing all right? You're looking a little pale.' Dr Manalo smiled at Maya, shaking her head amusedly.

'I think I'm doing okay.' Maya forced a laugh, embarrassment still warming her cheeks.

'Oh, really? A little birdie told me you were rushed to the university infirmary last night.' Dr. Manalo raised an eyebrow, a knowing smile gracing her lips.

'Oh. You know about that?' Maya searched through her mind for a reasonable explanation for what happened at the infirmary.

'Of course! You know how Islanders are. News spreads fast, but gossip spreads faster!' She laughed.

Maya shook her head amusedly. 'Right. I'm not entirely sure what happened either, but my younger sister found me unconscious in our apartment. It was a good thing she called the health services office and brought me to the infirmary right away.' The back of Maya's neck was heating up too. 'Otherwise, I don't know what would've happened to me.'

In the corner of her eye, the shadows by the bookshelf started moving again.

'Oh, I'm sure. Thank goodness your family was there to help you.' She started rifling through the pages of Maya's writing again, stopping at the sixth page and smiling. 'By the way, what deities did you include in these notes? Any interesting ones that I can tag as a priority for editing?'

Maya blinked at the sudden change in topic. 'Yes, of course.'

The shadow twisted around in its place, almost like it was panicking. It immediately started growing in size, and in a matter of moments, it was looming over them like a dark cloud.

Maya was careful not to stare. She wasn't sure what the shadow wanted this time, so she answered hesitantly. 'Like I mentioned, I included a bunch of stories about some lesser-known spirits that don't get talked about much in Islandic mythology, like Okot, Maklium, Anitun Tabun . . .' she trailed off, seeing that Dr Manalo was still smiling. In fact, she had not moved an inch. She seemed frozen in time.

'How wonderful,' Dr Manalo spoke, her smile never leaving her face. She was so eerily still that for a moment, Maya thought that she had stopped breathing.

Their eyes met, Maya's brown eyes with Dr Manalo's black ones, regarding each other in silence.

The shadow grew even bigger, enveloping the entire ceiling in darkness. It was trying to say something, but Maya didn't know what.

It felt like hours before Dr Manalo spoke again. 'Tell me, Maya. Have you ever heard of the legend of Bakunawa?'

At that, the shadow above their heads narrowed to a thin line. Then, it circled round and round on the ceiling.

It almost looked like a snake trying to catch its tail.

Maya froze. 'No, I haven't.' That was a lie.

'But you know so many of the folk tales of the Old World, my dear. I'm surprised you haven't heard of her. She was a very powerful spirit.' Dr Manalo stood up slowly, her smile still plastered on her face, the shadows in the office casting splotches of grey on her skin. 'She could go anywhere, do anything. The land and the sea were hers to command.' She licked her lips, smearing her red lipstick. 'But you know the one thing she never had command over? Her hunger. She was always hungry.'

The shadow on the ceiling was incessant now, quickening and increasing in speed as it spun around, the steady rhythm calling to her. *Like a warning.*

'It's a good thing she wasn't picky. She ate anything that would quell her appetite. Trees, lakes, rivers, mountains, all of it was food for her. And when she wasn't in the mood for the wonders of nature, well.' Her smile grew even wider. 'Human flesh would do.'

A chill ran down Maya's spine.

'But there was one thing in particular that she coveted the most.' Dr Manalo reached for the blinds covering the window behind her, pulling the cord to allow moonlight to flood the room. 'The one thing she still hadn't tasted.'

The full moon shone in the night sky. In the pale light, Maya could see Dr Manalo clearly now. Her eyes had turned a sickening yellow.

The shadow had stopped circling on the ceiling now and was back in the shape of a straight line. It pointed towards the door. *Get out.*

Maya slowly stood up from her chair. 'I think I need to go. Thank you for your time, Dr Manalo.' *Aga.* She had to get to Aga.

'Where are you going, *Mayari*?' Her smile continued to grow bigger, baring all of her teeth. 'I was just about to tell you about all those poor kids that disappeared. I finally have news to share with you.'

Maya looked down to see that Dr Manalo's nails had grown long and sharp. She dug them into the hardwood of her desk with a high-pitched grating sound that hurt Maya's ears.

'It seems that the police found some human remains in one of the city sewers connected to campus.' She laughed, a childish giggle that made the hairs on the back of Maya's neck stand up. 'They were identified to belong to one of the kids. Chan, I think. I remember her.'

Amanda. They had found Amanda Chan's remains.

Dr Manalo licked her lips. Her tongue darted out in between to taste the air. 'It's a shame that they all went missing. But oh, did they taste delicious.'

Maya's hand slowly crept up towards her chest, where the amulet Maxim had given her rested underneath the neckline of her dress.

'I bet you'll taste just as good.'

Her heart dropped. She felt her arm jerk to the side towards the door, as if someone had pulled her, telling her to run.

Dr Manalo's jaw unhinged, opening wide to let out a terrifying hiss before she lunged across the desk, claws outstretched towards Maya's throat.

Part II

Chapter 16

Maya flung herself to the left with a scream, rolling across the floor before scrambling back up on her knees.

Dr Manalo pivoted and kicked off from the closed office door, springing back towards her, fangs gleaming in the moonlight.

Maya threw her body to the right, hitting her shoulder on the wall with a hard thud, the plaster cracking from impact.

She watched in horror as Dr Manalo crawled towards her on all fours, her arms and legs bent at unnatural angles like a lizard's. Against the shadows, she could see her skin shedding off her face in pieces, her pupils narrowing into black slits against her yellow irises, and her long tongue darting in and out of her mouth, flicking against her fangs.

'*My dear Mayari.*' Her voice was a low, throaty growl now, the end of Maya's name ending in a hiss. 'In a university full of thousands of students, how lucky am I to have Kaylahon's next descendant come crawling to me?'

A guttural sound came from Dr Manalo, almost like she was laughing. 'You didn't even make me work hard to find you. How pathetic.'

Maya edged herself further to the right, closer towards the exit door. Her eyes darted to the right to gauge the distance.

'You're just in time for dinner. I haven't had a babaylan in so long, and I'm so very hungry.' Dr Manalo lunged again, faster than Maya could move out of the way.

Dr Manalo clamped her jaws around Maya's right ankle, sending a white-hot pain shooting up her leg.

Maya let out a bloodcurdling scream while Dr Manalo transformed into something more grotesque. Gone was her black hair, now melting into her back; her serpentine eyes had moved further back to the sides of her head; her nose lengthened into a snout. Her rosy skin rippled, now a murky dark green.

With her good foot, Maya kicked as hard as she could, aiming at the monster's eyes and nostrils. Her back hit the floor as it pulled her towards it, and her arms flailed for anything she could use as a weapon. Her hands closed around a heavy ceramic object, and without looking at it she hurled it at the monster's head with all of her strength.

The sea salt candle from Dr Manalo's table shattered against its head. It let out an irritated growl, its jaw loosening as it shook off the tiny broken bits falling into its eyes.

Maya felt its jaw lift from her flesh and made up her mind in an instant, bracing herself for what she was about to do.

With a pained cry, she pulled her right leg free, feeling her flesh tear open against the monster's teeth.

Liquid warmth spilled all over her leg. She looked down to see her bloodied ankle, torn open and leaking blood all over her shredded leather boot.

The monster shrieked and lunged for her again, but this time, Maya caught its open jaw with her left foot, the heel of her thick boot blocking its teeth from sinking into her flesh. She pulled her foot back and kicked as hard as she could, one fast strike after another before the monster reeled back in pain.

Maya crawled her way to the exit door, reaching up for the doorknob to try and pull herself up from the floor.

She managed to stand up on her left leg and brace herself against the door frame, her breathing laboured.

She was going to die.

She wasn't going to make it to Aga.

A shadow loomed over her from behind, and all the hairs on the back of her neck stood up.

She turned to look at the monster, now sanding at full height, its giant head pressing against the ceiling. It had transformed into its full serpentine form, the frills on its neck erect and fluttering, jaw wide enough to swallow Maya whole. It raised its body higher, poised to strike the final blow.

Bakunawa.

Maya put her hand over her heart to steady her breathing. If she died, let it be in peace as she accepted her fate.

Her hand brushed against the warm vibrating amulet on her chest.

Maxim's amulet rested around her neck, incessantly pulsing.

Bakunawa lunged at her. In that split second, Maya tore the amulet from her neck and smashed it on the ground, putting her hands up over her face and shutting her eyes, praying to whichever god was listening that she didn't misunderstand Maxim's instructions.

A burst of white light flooded the room.

When she opened her eyes, she was surrounded by a wall of the same white light, curving at the edges to close off at the walls of the office and seal her and the office door safely inside. Bakunawa shrieked, recoiling away from the wall.

Maya remembered that she still had her hand on the doorknob. Leaning all her weight on her left side, she twisted the door open, limping out into the hallway and collapsing on the ground.

She turned just in time to see Bakunawa claw at the wall of light, only for her arms to disappear each time. *A portal!*

Maya knew it wouldn't hold for long, not without Maxim to keep it up. Her eyes watered at the thought of Maxim rushing to help her, only to find her dead body strewn on the floor, or whatever was left of it after Bakunawa devoured her.

Two strong hands wound themselves tightly under her arms and pulled her up, startling her. She pushed away, accidentally leaning on her wounded right leg.

'Get away from me!' she cried out in pain, thrashing around wildly in an attempt to be free of whoever was holding her.

'Maya!' Aga placed his hands firmly on her shoulders to steady her. 'Maya, stop! It's me!'

Maya stopped throwing her arms around to look at Aga, who was running his warm hands up and down her arms, lines of worry creasing his forehead.

'What the tak is happening? I heard some noise coming from the other end of the hallway and . . .' his eyes travelled down to look at her bloody leg.

'Maya.' Aga eyes hardened. 'Who did this to you?'

'Aga,' Maya whimpered. 'We have to get out of here.'

'We need to get you to a hospital.' Aga's voice was a growl as he gently scooped Maya up into his arms. Her vision was swimming with black spots.

'Aga.' Maya's voice was weak as she tugged on his shirt.

Aga shook his head furiously as he walked down the hall. 'I've got you, don't worry. I'm not leaving you. I promise.'

The sound of splintering wood filled the hallway, followed by a vicious hiss. Aga turned around with Maya in his arms, only to come face to face with white fangs and an open jaw.

Aga screamed before dropping to his knees on the floor, still holding Maya firmly in his arms. Bakunawa's coiled body took up the entire hallway as she bobbed her giant head around, looking for them.

Aga slid with quick precision behind Bakunawa on his knees, slipping quietly underneath her head before standing up again on the other side of her. Maya clung desperately to him; her arms wrapped tightly around his neck as she forced herself not to feel any pain.

Bakunawa swung her giant head back towards them and struck, narrowly missing as Aga leaped to the side again, now in the clear and running down the hallway.

'What the tak,' Aga muttered to himself. 'What the tak. What the tak.'

'*Agatzuki Kaneko*,' the monster's chilling voice called out to them.

Aga turned around slowly with Maya still in his arms. Bakunawa was slithering down the hall, right towards them.

'Aga, run.' Maya tugged on his shirt again, her voice pleading. 'Please, we need to run.'

Aga's eyes darted around the faculty centre, but his body remained rooted in place.

Bakunawa approached almost lazily, as if she knew that the two couldn't outrun her.

'Oh my, what a treat this night will be.' A laughing hiss escaped from her open mouth, her tongue flicking at the air.

She lifted herself up, jaws open and fangs glistening in the light, ready to devour them both.

Aga pressed his lips to Maya's hair, and for a second, she thought that he was kissing her goodbye.

She closed her eyes to savour the feeling of his warmth against her.

'I'm going to throw you,' he whispered.

Maya's eyes flew open before Aga flung her to the side, sliding her across the floor to the opposite side of the room.

She felt another burst of pain shoot up her injured leg as she hit the opposite wall. She lifted her leg up, to see that her sock and pant leg were entirely soaked with blood.

She turned back to scream at Aga to run, to get help, to leave her behind.

He was doing the complete opposite.

Aga had taken one of the wooden swords displayed on the wall behind him and was holding it in place between Bakunawa's fangs, forcing her jaw open and pushing her back with all his strength.

Bakunawa hissed loudly, looming over Aga and pushing down on him, her tongue flicking wildly at his face and hair.

Aga groaned under the pressure, his arms shaking as Bakunawa pushed him down to his knees.

'Aga!' Maya screamed at him. 'The other sword!'

Aga looked across the room at her only for a second, giving her the barest hint of a smile before he let go, quickly jumping out of the way before she slammed into the floor with the wooden sword still in her mouth.

Quickly, Aga swiped the other wooden sword off its rack on the wall and swung it down on Bakunawa's head, slamming the sword down with all his might.

He hit her again and again, bringing the sword down on her eyes and nostrils, the sound of wood slapping hard on scales before Bakunawa ceased moving altogether. Blood splattered all over the floor.

Aga was breathing hard, the sword still hovering above his head when he stopped. He looked down at the giant unmoving serpent, then back at Maya, who was looking at him in shock.

Aga took a step back, the sword clattering noisily to the ground. He put a hand on his heart, clutching at the fabric that covered it, before slowly making his way towards Maya.

From her curled up position against the wall, Maya could see Aga's shaking hands. There was blood all over his white button-up and glasses. He looked like he had just seen a ghost.

'Are you okay?' he breathed out.

Despite herself, Maya managed to let out a gurgling laugh, tears pricking at the corners of her eyes. 'Yeah.'

Aga took a few slow steps towards her. Maya sat up and leaned against the wall, careful not to jostle her right leg.

She wanted to stand up and limp towards Aga, maybe even hug him for saving her life. She looked up at him and smiled, until she spotted a shadow moving in the corner of her eye.

Just in time to see Bakunawa rising up over Aga, her frills shaking and her jaw wide open.

Bakunawa lunged, her mouth aiming for Aga's neck.

In Maya's eyes, everything happened in slow motion.

Aga turned around, his face paling before he cried out Maya's name.

Maya threw herself in Aga's direction, trying to grab him as Bakunawa's open mouth moved in closer.

A blinding light appeared in front of them, shielding Bakunawa from view. Maya heard an agonized scream.

Maxim stepped out from the wall of light, a look of desperation on their face as they grabbed Aga and Maya by their shirts and pulled them towards the light.

The harsh lights of the faculty centre and the sound of Bakunawa's scream faded away into darkness.

Maya felt her head slam down against a hard surface. She heard Aga moaning beside her. She reached her hand out towards the sound, feeling around for him until her fingers closed around the soft fabric of his shirt.

'Aga,' she whispered his name.

'Maya, keep your eyes open,' Maxim's voice called out to her, softer than it was before. She tried to form words, but her tongue was heavy in her mouth. She felt the darkness surrounding her.

She let herself fall into it.

Chapter 17

'Please,' Hanan bit her lip to keep it from quivering, 'you don't understand. She's in danger.'

Officer Hererra's smile was full of pity. 'I recognize your concern, Ms. Halili. But like I said. I can't file an official report until it's been at least twenty-four hours.' He looked up at the wall clock behind him. 'And it's only been five.'

Hanan nodded silently, unable to come up with another response. At one in the morning, the Santa Teresita police station was nearly empty, save for her and a few other sleepy police officers.

Officer Herrera closed his notebook and clasped his hands together under his stubbly chin. 'Listen, I know you're worried about your sister, but let's not jump to conclusions, *ha?* Who knows, she might be spending time with her friends. Maybe she's out with a handsome gentleman.' He raised his eyebrows suggestively.

Hanan pushed down the bile rising in her throat. It had taken everything in her to leave the apartment she shared with Maya and come here. Her skin itched at the thought of begging for help from authority. Now she knew it had been a mistake.

She knew Maya was in danger. She felt the wrongness deep in her bones, a pulsating energy that sent shivers down her spine. She knew to trust it now after everything that happened.

All you have to know is that it's not you they're looking for.

Hanan tried her best to block out the hurt that followed each time she remembered what Maxim had said. There was a small part of her that wished Maxim had talked to her instead, that the spirits had chosen *her*. She had so many questions for them. Why only now? Why did it have to be their family?

Why was *Maya* the only one with power?

'Ms Halili?' Officer Herrera's voice interrupted her thoughts.

Hanan looked down at her hands to see them balled up in her skirt. She locked eyes with Officer Herrera, whose brows furrowed in concern.

She stood up abruptly. 'Thank you for your time, officer. I'll take it from here.' She turned on her heel and walked towards the exit door without looking back.

She didn't need their help. She would find Maya on her own.

She slipped quietly out of the police station and into the night.

Chapter 18

When Aga opened his eyes again, he was burning.

He blinked once, twice, very slowly as soft light and the scent of cinnamon flooded his senses. His skin felt like it was on fire. *Was this what the afterlife smelled like?*

He sat up, his back cracking in ten different places as he took in his surroundings. He was on a green couch in the middle of a modestly sized apartment, with pillows of all different sizes and colours stacked behind him and under his feet. The fading light from outside told him it was the late afternoon.

'Yeah, I see him,' a gruff female voice said from behind. She spoke in a brusque language that took Aga a few moments to recognize. 'Let him wake up on his own.' It was Umani, from the neighbouring island west of Kinadman.

Aga turned around to see an odd-looking group of individuals seated at the round dining table. There were four of them in total, including Maxim, who was sipping on a mug of steaming liquid in silence, eyeing him carefully.

They wore the plain linen clothing of middle-class Islanders, though some of them looked like they hadn't changed in a few days. Each of them had the same glowing orb around their necks.

A young man with tawny skin spoke first. 'He looks like tak.' His Umani was loud and booming. It reverberated through Aga's sensitive temples.

Another young man with dark hair and grey eyes hit him on the arm. He looked younger, closer to a boy than a man, and his complexion was cool and pale against his thin frame. 'Don't be rude,' he said quietly in a different language. Aga combed through his third-year lessons, trying to place the boy's words before finally landing on Bulosi, from the northwestern Island.

'I'm not being rude if it's the truth,' the tawny-skinned man quickly replied in Bulosi. 'Gods, I can't say anything these days.' He ran a hand through the ringlets cropped close to his scalp and cursed under his breath. Aga could've sworn that his eyes pulsed with a bright red glow.

'Nacio,' the woman across the table from them warned. She was the owner of the gruff voice from earlier, Aga realized. Half of her long, dark hair was swept to the side, the other half completely shaven. Strange markings were etched into the short side of her hair alongside a string of tattoos that ran from her temple to the back of her head. She stared at Aga, unblinking.

'Hawi started it,' Nacio mumbled under his breath in Umani.

The pale boy named Hawi scoffed. 'Flor knows better than to listen to you.'

'Flor is right here.' Flor ran a hand down her face and groaned.

'Maybe we shouldn't fight in front of our guest. It leaves a bad impression.' Hawi looked pointedly at Aga. 'Ignore them. How are you feeling?'

Aga opened his mouth to speak, but nothing came out. He had no idea what to say to these strange-looking people.

'What, is he mute or something?' Nacio raised an eyebrow at him.

From their side of the table, Maxim laughed. 'Definitely not.'

'I think he's in shock.' Maxim put down their empty mug and stood up from the table. 'Also, I can feel Alon hovering outside like a creep. I'll get the door.'

Aga rubbed his eyes and patted down the cushions around him to look for his glasses. He found them folded and placed neatly on the side table to his left. He looked down at his body to see that he was still wearing his white button-down. He had a big tear in his left pant leg, and he was also missing a sock, but the rest of his body still seemed to be intact.

Aga cleared his throat, feeling the dryness in his tongue. 'Maya,' he said, testing her name out in his mouth, 'where is Maya?' he spoke cautiously in Kinadmani.

Nacio smirked at him and rolled his eyes. 'Relax, lover boy. She's resting in the bedroom.'

Aga tried to stand up from the couch before flopping right back down and wincing in pain.

'Sit down,' Hawi ordered gently. 'She'll be with us in a bit.'

Hawi stood up from the table and took a few steps into the kitchenette. He pulled the kettle from the stove, pouring Aga a mug of whatever they were drinking. 'Here,' he said as he handed it to Aga.

Aga thanked him before staring down at the mug in his hands. The hot liquid inside warmed his fingers as he wrapped them around the mug's body. He took a sip, letting it flow and wet his aching throat. It burned deliciously on his tongue and in his nose. He took a few more gulps before setting the empty mug down before him.

Hawi's voice was barely above a whisper as he spoke to the others, 'I still think we need to give them more time to recover. He's definitely still not all right.'

Aga gulped. Right. The giant snake who turned out to be Dr Manalo. Or was it the other way around? Whatever it was, it had tried to eat them. It had tried to *kill them*.

He cleared his throat again before speaking up. 'Where are we?' He pointed at his mug. 'And may I please have some more of this?'

Hawi hummed in response as he picked up Aga's mug and walked back into the kitchen for a refill. 'It's salabat. It's good for your throat. And pretty much everything else.'

He stretched out his legs before slowly standing up from his spot on the sofa. His gaze wandered around the dimly lit apartment, taking note of all the colourful pillows, rugs, and delicately woven items decorating the space. Despite the small area, it felt warm and lived-in, like someone had been calling it home for a long time.

'We're in Maxim's apartment. Well, one of them,' Nacio responded. He pointed across the room at the owner in question, who was letting a hooded figure in through the front door. The new guest moved silently across the floorboards towards the others, not even sparing a glance at Aga. His black jacket completely engulfed him, and his hood covered half his face. Aga caught a glimpse of dark brown skin and full lips.

Alon sat down at the dining table without a word, wrapping his hands around his own mug. Hawi turned to him with a smile, making a quick hand gesture in greeting. Alon mirrored the gesture before taking a sip of salabat.

'Don't mind Alon.' Maxim came up behind Aga and clapped him gently on the back before leaning in closer to whisper in his ear. 'He's shy around strangers. You'll learn how to talk to him soon enough.'

'No, he won't,' Flor replied sharply. Her Kinadmani was fluid and natural. 'Not until we figure out our next steps. You still haven't answered any of our questions about this boy, Maxim. Who is he, and why did you bring him here?' She brought down her hand on the table with a loud thump. 'It was only supposed to be *her*.'

Maxim's grip on Aga's shoulder tightened. 'Plans change, Flor. I couldn't just leave him there. He would've died.'

Flor laughed bitterly. 'And what about us? Look at him.' She pointed an accusing finger at Aga. 'He's a foreigner, for tak's sake. How do we know he won't run straight to the Astyrians and report us? He's seen our faces already.' She turned to him now, seething. 'He'll get us killed.'

'But he saved Maya's life!' Hawi protested.

'So what?' Nacio piped in. 'That doesn't mean he'll save ours.'

'Then why don't you just ask him?' Maxim challenged.

The room fell silent. All eyes turned to him.

Aga weighed his options.

If he spoke candidly and told them that he didn't want to be involved, they could kill him. Not the most ideal scenario.

If he lied and played along, they could spare him. He could continue with his little mission, collect even more valuable information for his father, and win his freedom.

But what about Maya?

Information in exchange for freedom, his father's voice echoed in his mind. *Do this, and I will cut you loose. I will set you free.*

But the only thing he was thinking of was Maya, scared and wounded, calling out to him.

Aga cleared his throat. He knew that the next words that came out of his mouth would decide his fate. He decided a mix of lies and truth would fit best.

'I won't,' Aga spoke in clear Kinadmani. 'I swear I won't report you.' He turned to Flor, whose unsettling eyes bore deep into him. He switched to Umani, though he knew his accent was atrocious. 'This is my home, the same way it is yours.' He turned to Hawi, this time in Bulosi. 'And I hate the Astyrians just as much as you do. I care for the Islands as much as you do.' He turned to Nacio. 'And I care about Maya. I won't betray you any more than I would betray her. I don't understand what you're doing, but,' he glanced at Alon, 'I'm willing to help in whatever way I can.'

The five of them stared at Aga for a few beats of silence. Then, Nacio scoffed. 'Okay, show-off.'

Maxim let out a low whistle. 'Didn't know you had it in you, boy.' They chuckled. 'Whatever I was expecting, it definitely wasn't that.'

'Same.' Hawi wrapped his thin arms around his even thinner waist, shivering against a phantom breeze. 'That was impressive, albeit a little creepy. How do you know so many Islander languages? Aren't you . . .' He gestured vaguely at Aga. 'What are you, exactly?'

'Kiruvian.' Aga looked down at his feet. 'And I was a linguistics major.'

'Ah,' Hawi said hesitantly, 'definitely a little creepy.'

'And why did you decide to move here?' Nacio raised an eyebrow. 'Why the Seven Islands, of all places?'

Aga was prepared for this line of questioning. He had answered the same questions numerous times in his first year here.

'The weather, mostly,' Aga replied. 'It gets really cold in Kiru. And they're not big on learning foreign languages over there. I figured I had a better chance of expanding my horizons if I studied in a place that offered multiple opportunities to learn.'

Nacio rolled his eyes. 'Nerd.'

'Have you been to other places in the Islands?' Hawi offered.

'No, but I've always wanted to visit Hiwaga,' Aga spoke truthfully. 'I hear their beaches are beautiful.'

'That's a shame. Maya's from Hiwaga.' Maxim walked around him towards the kitchen. They picked up a dirty, blackened pan from the sink and sighed. 'Speaking of which, I think we should probably get Maya. We need to have an important conversation with her.'

Flor and Alon were silent. Flor's eyes were now trained at the eastern wall of the apartment, her lower lip caught in between her teeth. Alon remained motionless in his seat, his hood still over his head.

'Can I use your telephone?' Aga tried. 'I'd like to give my roommate a call to let them know why I didn't come home last night.' Aga didn't have a roommate. 'I'll just make something up, so he doesn't worry.'

Maxim gestured towards the door at the end of the narrow hallway. 'Be my guest.' They followed behind Aga and stopped in front of the second door to the left. They turned back around and called to the others at the dining table, 'I'll talk to Maya. Try not to kill each other while you're at it.'

'No promises,' Flor muttered.

Chapter 19

Maya sat cross-legged on Maxim's bed. Her bottom lip was raw from chewing on it for the past hour, and her nails were bitten down to the quick.

Hanan hadn't answered her calls to their apartment in the last three hours. She had tried calling the front desk, but their building security guard hadn't seen her come in or out of the building since last night.

'I'm sorry, ma'am,' Ate Sel had said. 'Last I saw her, she was on her way up to your unit. Haven't seen her since.'

Maya was desperate to know where Hanan was. After everything that happened to her and Aga, she was unsure of just how much danger she was in. If Dr Manalo—*Bakunawa*—knew who she was, it was only a matter of time before they found out about Hanan.

The sound of the bedroom door creaking open stole Maya's attention. Maxim stood in the doorway, an apologetic smile on their face.

Maya sighed and closed her eyes, her entire body sagging. 'Maxim.' She rubbed her forehead with her palm. 'Hi.'

She leaned back on the twin-sized mattress positioned on the floor. A stack of medical textbooks served as a nightstand, with the phone and a plain reading lamp on top of it. The only other furniture were two clothing racks, both full of colourful, billowy clothes. Maya was surprised by how normal and cozy Maxim's place was, and she wondered how much time they had to actually rest here with everything else going on.

She eyed her right ankle, encased in tight bandages. For the amount of damage it had suffered, it didn't hurt as bad as she thought it would. Maxim was an excellent doctor. She would just have to walk with a slight limp for the next few weeks.

Maxim shrugged. 'It's fine. Sorry for interrupting. I should've knocked.' They pointed a thumb out the door. 'Are you feeling all right? Because the others are waiting. They'd really like to talk to you.'

'The others?' Maya sat up straighter on the bed. 'They're here?' Maya had heard voices outside ever since she gained consciousness a few hours ago, but she had been too scared to go outside on her own.

Maxim nodded. 'They're in the kitchen.' They pressed their lips together, the corners of their mouth lifting. 'So is Aga.'

'Aga's still here?' Maya felt herself sitting up straighter. 'How is he?'

Maxim's smile grew. 'He's fine. He woke up a while ago. First thing he asked about was you.'

Maya chewed on her lip as she felt the blood rushing to her cheeks, her eyes looking anywhere but at Maxim. She could not let them see her blushing because of Aga Kaneko, of all people. She let out a long, slow breath. 'I have no idea how we're going to do this. I don't even feel tethered to my own body right now. Everything is so . . .' she gestured wildly at the space around her, 'up in the air. I have ten different trains of thought running through my mind right now.' Her hands came up to cover her face as she let out a low groan. 'It's always been like this in my head. I just wish I could just turn it all off.'

Maya always had a difficult time sorting through the mess in her mind. She thought that calling home would help her make sense of everything, but it had only given her more to worry about. Talking things out with her sister always helped, but knowing that anything she said to her could put them in further danger made her feel ten times worse.

'I don't know,' she trailed off. 'It's so noisy in my head.'

Maxim took a few steps forward and sat down beside Maya on the bed. 'I can't imagine what you're feeling right now. My experience entering all of this . . .' they flailed their arms around in the air, making Maya laugh, '. . . was a lot different than yours. I'm sorry that things are happening this way. Everything is moving so quickly.' They paused, a small smile creeping up their face. 'But I wasn't kidding when I said that we've been waiting for you. We need you, Maya. So, let's talk.'

Maya sighed. 'All right. Let's do it.'

They made their way out of the bedroom towards the loud chorus of voices in the kitchen. 'Don't worry, they're good people,' Maxim reassured her. 'You'll love them.'

Maya held her breath, anxious to see the faces of the others like her.

She rounded the corner and was greeted by a blazing wall of fire.

'This sounds like a trick.'

'I have no reason to lie to you, tado-oya.' Aga clenched his jaw against the telephone. 'It's the truth.'

Masaki Kaneko was silent on the other end of the line. 'If what you're saying is true, that supernatural creatures and powerful beings are indigenous to the Seven Islands, then this could work splendidly in our favour.' For the first time in his life, Aga heard excitement in his father's voice. 'Of course, I'll still have to send in an undercover unit to verify your reports. It's a shame what happened to Kenji.' The way his father said it made Aga feel like he didn't actually care. 'General Ito will be pleased to hear about this.' He paused. 'You've done well, son.'

Aga felt sick to his stomach at the praise. 'What are you planning to do with this information, anyway?'

'That's none of your concern.' His father said dismissively. 'All you need to do is stay with the shamans and keep collecting information. Once our plans are in action, I'll make sure to clear your name with the Astyrians.'

'What?' Aga asked sharply. 'Why would the Astyrians be involved?'

'Just shut up and do what you're told,' Masaki replied coldly. 'You're in no position to question or argue.'

Aga let out a deep breath. 'Fine.'

'Call me again in a week. I'll be expecting a more detailed update.' The line went dead.

Aga slammed the receiver back into the telephone. He rubbed at his temples, thinking about what he was doing.

What exactly was he doing?

He was selling out the babaylan to Kiru in exchange for his freedom.

He swallowed, shaking his head.

There was no saving him from what he'd already done. He would either have to live with his decisions or let them kill him.

He quietly slipped out of the bedroom and back into the main living area. He heard the raised voices before he saw them.

As he rounded the corner, he saw that Nacio and Flor were standing face to face, their eyes glowing with crimson and green light.

Then the living room exploded.

Chapter 20

On the other side of the burning flames, Maya screamed.

Aga watched in horror as Nacio doubled over, his hands clutched to his chest, his eyes glowing a fiery red. Flor was shouting, telling everyone to back away.

It happened out of nowhere. One second, Nacio and Flor were standing off. The next thing Aga knew, Nacio had crushed the mug in his hands into dust and unknowingly summoned fire from the gas pipes in the wall. He stood up with a scream, pulling at his hair and clothes like he was trying to claw himself free from something. From *someone.*

'Nacio, that's enough!' Flor shouted, her eyes pulsing with green light. She towered over the rest of them, her palms out towards Nacio, who was now writhing in pain on the floor.

'Just give him a minute!' Hawi yelled back. To Aga's surprise, the gangly boy jumped from his seat to stand in front of the other babaylan. There were storms in his eyes as he spoke in a cold voice. 'He has it under control.'

Nacio groaned in pain as he pressed his palms into his eye sockets. 'Stop,' he moaned. 'Get out of my head.'

'Nacio, get it together!' Flor yelled at him. 'Gods, where is Alon?'

In the corner of the room, Alon immediately sprang into action. Aga watched in astonishment as the babaylan flipped across the table towards the sink in one fluid motion, his eyes glowing with a soft blue light. He quickly turned the sink on to its full pressure before thrusting his hands towards it, grasping on to thin air as if holding on to an invisible rope. Alon pulled at the air, and gushing water slowly redirected itself from the sink towards him.

'Faster, Alon.' Flor's tone was panicked as she looked towards the fire at the mouth of the hallway. The flames licked at the beams of the apartment's ceiling. Aga took a step back towards the front door.

'Just let him get a hold on it!' Hawi continued to yell, his eyes darkening. The sky outside the apartment windows rumbled with thunder, and the once blue hue quickly faded to a stormy grey. 'He can do it.'

'You know he can't, Hawi!' Flor pointed outside at the sky. 'And neither can you. Reel them in, *now*!' she barked at him. Flor turned back to Alon, who was balancing a stream of moving water in the air. 'Alon, do it!'

Alon took a few steps towards Nacio and Hawi, his arms gliding gracefully through the air. He took a step forward and the water stream followed him, dancing above everyone's heads. He pushed both of his hands together as if catching an invisible ball, and the water quickly responded by swirling itself into a sphere.

Aga couldn't believe his eyes. A ball of floating water was about to extinguish a wall of fire. Inside of an apartment.

With one strong push in Nacio's direction, the water whizzed past Flor and Hawi before dropping itself onto Nacio, completely soaking him.

Nacio gasped for air with one hand on his throat. Hawi clapped him hard on his back as he continued to cough and spit out water. Aga noticed that his eyes were no longer red.

He turned back to the hallway in time to see Maxim and Maya passing through the black scorch marks on the hardwood floor.

Maya looked a little shaken, but stood tall with resolve, taking in the strangers standing in the kitchen. Maxim crossed their arms and sighed. 'Is Nacio all right?'

Nacio slowly got up, leaning on Hawi's side. The two of them looked chastised. 'Yeah, I'm fine.' He spat out another mouthful of water. 'I have it under control.'

Flor took a step towards the pair and squared her shoulders. 'No, you don't. Maklium is obviously playing with you. He knows it's been months since you last went back for a *mutya.*' She enunciated each word with a finger pointed at Nacio, 'Keep. It. Together.'

'Just stop it, Flor,' Hawi snapped back. 'It's been a rough day. We'll help him get a new mutya after all of this is over.' He helped Nacio hobble back to a seat at the dining table, plopping him ungracefully into his chair. Alon watched everything in silence from his position beside the sink.

They all looked at each other, an uneasy silence descending on them all. One by one, they all turned to look at Maya, who remained standing in the middle of the hallway.

If Aga thought hard enough about everything he had just witnessed, he probably would have broken down on the spot. But Aga could see the resolve set in Maya's jaw, and the calm focus she had as she regarded each person in the kitchen. Her eyes locked with his, and he gave her the tiniest of smiles.

The corner of her lip lifted in response.

'Hello,' she said, her voice soft but clear, 'I'm Maya. Maxim told me about you.' She turned to look at Maxim with a raised eyebrow. 'But clearly not enough.'

Maxim let out an awkward laugh. 'Right, well. Now that we're all here, I think it's time for us to get right down to business. We don't have a lot of time, so let's make it quick.' Maxim pulled a chair from the dining table and twisted it around before taking a seat to face Maya. 'I know you've got a lot of questions, so fire away.'

Maya cleared her throat. 'Okay.' She took a deep breath. 'Who are you?'

Maxim spread their hands wide. 'We are the Hand of Kaylahon. There's five of us, each descended from the bloodlines of the babaylan who dedicated their lives in service to Kaylahon, the first babaylan.'

'We are the living bridges between this realm and the gods,' Hawi spoke. 'And we keep the rituals and traditions of the Old World alive.'

Maya shuffled her feet around on the floor. 'Okay, so there's five of you already. Where do I fit into all of this?'

Hawi gasped. 'She really doesn't know.'

'Quiet, you,' Flor snapped at Hawi before she took a step forward. 'Sorry about all of this. I know that these are less than ideal circumstances. I'm Flor.' She stuck her hand out towards Maya. 'Dumakulem's ward.'

Maya's eyes widened. 'Dumakulem . . . god of the earth?'

Flor pressed her lips together, almost as if she were holding back a smile. 'You're already way more prepared than I was when I first started.'

'What's a ward?' Maya asked.

'Each of us has a special connection to one or two gods, which we inherited after we came of age and took over the role from our predecessors. Dumakulem is my god. He's the one I call on.'

Maya turned to Maxim. 'Back at the university infirmary. You were opening portals. Which god allows you to do that?'

'Anagolay, goddess of lost things.' Maxim crossed their legs. 'That mutya I gave you to wear around your neck was infused with my blood. It was both a protection and location spell, courtesy of Anagolay.' They opened up their palm, revealing a glowing orb of light. Aga knew that if he tried to touch it, his hand would disappear into somewhere else entirely. 'When you broke it, I felt it in my blood, and I knew you were in trouble.' They gestured to the apartment around them. 'Pulled you through that light portal with as much life essence as I could spare. It's a miracle I got there in time.'

Maya didn't respond. 'So, whose ward am I?'

Hawi's face took on a reverential look. 'Kaylahon herself.'

'But how is that possible?' Maya demanded.

'After defeating Bakunawa one thousand years ago, the father of all things Bathala warned Kaylahon that Bakunawa would one day come back and finish what she started. In exchange for their bravery and loyalty to their gods and their people, Bathala promised Kaylahon and her loyal followers that their powers would be passed through their bloodlines, ensuring that there would always be blessed children to protect the Seven Islands.'

'So that's me,' Maya replied quietly. 'I'm Kaylahon's heir.'

Aga watched as her eyes dropped to her right ankle. He remembered her limping and bleeding, seeing her flesh torn so deeply that white bone had shone through the red. Aga had carried her and watched her blood drip down his arms.

Maxim's eyes pulsed with white light. 'You are. And with you, the Hand of Kaylahon will finally be at its full power. We haven't had a Kaylahon heir in fifteen years.' They gestured at the rest of the babaylan. 'This will be the first time that our connections to the spirit world will be strong and unbreakable. No more incidents like Nacio's earlier.'

'Hey,' Nacio grumbled.

'But it's true,' Flor joined in. 'With you, our connections to our gods will stabilize, and our powers will only double in reach and strength. You are the missing piece, Maya. We can't do this without you.'

'But why?' Maya demanded. 'Why *me*?'

'We don't get to choose the bloodline we are born into.' Flor's voice turned hard. 'We can only choose what we do with the blood given to us.'

'Is that why Bakunawa targeted me?' Maya's voice was quiet now. 'Is that why she pretended to be my friend? Because of my blood?'

Flor had the decency to look a little guilty. Maxim jumped in, saving her from having to reply. 'Yes, Maya. We don't know how she did it, but she managed to infiltrate the country's most prestigious university and latch on to you.'

'We've been looking for her ever since we felt the giant loss of energy in Kasanaan,' Hawi said. 'That big of a shift can't go unnoticed, especially by our gods.'

'We also caught wind of all the missing students in Kinadman,' Flor finally replied. 'We figured this is where she must have gone, so we followed her. She was probably drawn to your energy and took a chance at NUSI. She's been eating more innocent people and gathering her strength since then.' She pointed at the pale rays of moonlight just starting to shine through the window. 'And she's not going to stop until she gets what she came for.' She pointed back at her. 'That includes you.'

Aga watched as Maya's face flicked through multiple different emotions at once. Shock, confusion, then anger, then sadness. Her brows knit together as she balled her fists by her sides.

'This is insane. You all sound *insane.*' She took another deep breath. 'But I trust you. Just tell me what I have to do.'

'We leave Kinadman. It's not safe here any more.' Maxim stood, turning back to the kitchen and picking up what looked like a collection of random things in their arms. A bag of tea leaves. Oranges. A serrated knife with an intricately carved wooden handle.

'The next most important thing you need to do is the initiation ritual,' Hawi said. 'The best and safest place to do it is in our home base. We'll be taking a high-speed ferry there tonight and avoid getting caught by any more of Bakunawa's minions.'

Maxim pointed at them with the tip of their knife. 'It's clear that Bakunawa knew exactly who you were. She was just biding her time until we found you.' They waved the knife around their midsection. 'And now she knows that we're here, too. It's only a matter of time before she finds us.' They pulled out a giant woven sack from behind the refrigerator and threw the contents of their arms into it. 'She's going to take and destroy as much as she needs to in order to get what she wants. She's not going to stop until she plunges our entire world into darkness.' Maxim pulled out a few more things from the kitchen drawers. 'That's why demons like Mangaway are helping her. They'll have free reign of our world once darkness overtakes it.'

They plopped the gigantic woven bag on to the dining table and rested a hand on their hip. 'I'll help you file a leave of absence at school. We'll send a letter to your family in Hiwaga. Maybe something along the lines of a deadly infectious disease. I'm a doctor, so I can vouch for you.'

'Wait a minute,' Maya held up her hands helplessly, 'I can't just drop everything here in Kinadman.' Aga could hear the desperation in her voice. She turned to look at him. 'What about Aga? What about our jobs?'

'Forget about it.' Nacio piped in, standing up to help Maxim pack things into another sack bag. 'Forget about your life here in Kinadman. The most important thing you need to do right now is do the initiation ritual. Once your powers awaken, you'll stand a better chance of defending yourself.'

Maya put her face in her hands, groaning. 'This is impossible. I have the rest of my life to think about! What about my family? What about Hanan?' Aga could tell that she was angry now. This entire thing sounded so incredibly dangerous, and Aga still wasn't sure if he believed in any of it, but he couldn't imagine what was going on in Maya's mind right now.

'This isn't what I want. This,' Maya pointed at Maxim, 'is not what I want to be.'

Anger flashed in Maxim's eyes. 'I think you're still under the impression that you have a choice in this matter, so let me make this very clear. You don't.'

Flor stood beside Maya, forming an impenetrable wall and making her back up. 'The spirits have made contact with you, and Bakunawa is going to try and get to you before you go through with the ritual. We have to do it, or else you'll be putting yourself and everyone around you in danger.'

'What ritual?' Maya sounded so tired. 'This is my life you're talking about! I can't just leave! I can't . . .' she trailed off, her eyes glistening. 'You can't make me do this.'

Aga took a few steps towards Maya and reached for her. 'Maya?' She was crying now. It pained him to see her so upset.

'Don't you get it?' Maxim raised their voice. 'You won't have a life if Bakunawa *kills you first*!'

They were interrupted by a knock at the door.

Chapter 21

Maya's chaotic thoughts were abruptly interrupted by the sound of knuckles on wood.

Aga stopped in his tracks, letting his hand fall back down to his side. Maya was almost disappointed that he did. 'I'll get it.' He turned to open the front door.

He was immediately pulled back by Maxim, whose jaw was clenched.

Maxim let out a long breath before straightening up and pointing two fingers at Maya and Aga. 'You two. Inside my bedroom. Now.'

'Excuse me?' Maya squeaked out.

Her mind was still reeling from their heated exchange, and now they were ordering them around like children. Maxim was already on their way to the front door.

'Hey, I'm talking to you! What's going on?' Maya yelled at them. She felt a warm hand on her forearm and turned to see Aga, eyebrows pressed together, subtly shaking his head.

Maxim stopped dead in their tracks. Without turning back, they said, 'I'm not going to ask again. In the bedroom, *now*.'

Silently, the other four babaylan took positions around the apartment. Alon stayed beside the sink, while Hawi and Flor stood beside the windows. Nacio walked with them down the hallway, turning back every few seconds to look at the front door. He gently pushed them into the bedroom.

'Stay put and lock this door,' he ordered. 'Do not open it for anything or anyone. Doesn't matter if we beg or plead with you to open it. Maxim has a key, so we'll open it ourselves.' Nacio's grip on the doorknob was tight as he slammed the door shut.

Maya could feel her own blood boiling in her veins. Her mind was a complete mess of thoughts, and she had no idea what to make of it. They were shutting her out seconds after begging her to join them. They were keeping her safe from a potentially harmful situation. They were testing her.

Maya decided to ignore Nacio's warning and got down on her knees to crack the bedroom door slightly ajar, enough for her to see outside and down the hallway.

'What are you doing?' Aga whispered angrily. 'Nacio said to lock the door!'

'We're safe as long as we're inside. And don't tell me you're not even the tiniest bit curious,' Maya whispered back. 'I'll lock the door if things get messy.'

'I'm not curious! I'm the opposite of curious!' Aga continued to whisper-yell. 'Close the door, Halili. I don't want to see what happens if we don't.'

She turned back to glare at him. 'Or what, Kaneko?'

They stared at each other for a few heartbeats, neither of them backing down. Maya took note of the way Aga's glasses sat slightly askew on his face since the last time she saw him. His borrowed shirt was entirely too big for him, and his cheeks were flushed pink.

Aga is handsome. The thought crossed Maya's mind quicker than she could form it. She frowned and bit her lip.

Aga's eyes trailed down her face to settle on her mouth. His own lips parted, ready to respond. Instead, he sighed, turning away to run his hands through his hair and groan. 'So impulsive,' he muttered.

Maya shook her head free from thoughts of Aga's attractiveness, turning back to the door. From behind her, she felt Aga crouch slightly by the wall next to the door frame, his chin resting slightly on the top of her head. His one arm rested on the door itself, caging Maya in and enveloping her in his warm, musky scent.

Maya cracked the bedroom door open a little more and peeked through the sliver of light. Nacio was standing on the scorched wood in front of the hallway, his stocky frame taking up almost all of the space in the entry. At the other end of the apartment, she watched as Maxim opened the front door with the deadbolt chain still attached, but their towering figure blocked Maya from seeing who was behind it. The gentle voice of a woman sounded from the door.

'Good evening,' the woman said. Her voice was light and sweet, and barely audible from across the room. She sounded young. 'I'm Maria, your upstairs neighbour on the sixth floor. I just moved in last week. Very sorry to be bothering you at this time of night, but I just got back from a trip to Gahum to visit family and I have many heavy bags with me.'

'Where are your bags?' Maxim asked.

'They're over there at the bottom of the stairs. I made it all the way to the fourth floor, but I don't think I can carry it all the way to the sixth.' A nervous giggle.

'My apologies, but perhaps you can ask for help from another neighbour.'

Maya raised her eyebrows at Maxim's strange response. The lady only needed help with her bags, and Maxim was more than capable of carrying them up to the next floor.

'I assure you it will only take a couple of minutes.'

Maya watched Nacio tense up. She heard the ice in Maxim's voice when they replied, 'Sorry, I can't. Good evening.' They grasped at the knob to close the door.

The woman's hand shot out to grab at Maxim's sleeve. Maya noticed Hawi opening the window, his hand faced upwards towards the sky.

'Please,' the woman begged. She sounded close to tears. 'I really need your help. You wouldn't turn down a woman in need, would you?'

Maya watched as Maxim stood taller, rising to their full height as their top bun grazed the door frame. They gripped the door frame tightly before speaking in a low, threatening tone.

'My upstairs neighbour is an old man in his eighties who asks me to water his plants every week.' Maxim leaned forward towards the small opening in the doorway. 'I don't know who you think you're fooling, but you're not my upstairs neighbour, and you're not a woman in need.

I'm going to give you five seconds to walk away before you regret ever coming here.'

The woman was silent for a few seconds before letting out a dark chuckle. She withdrew her long, spindly fingers from Maxim's forearm. 'Silly me. Must have knocked on the wrong door. Enjoy the rest of your evening.'

Maxim slammed the door in the woman's face whose eerie giggles slowly faded from the hallway. They turned the lock and backed away quickly. Their hands shook as they bumped into the side table beside the couch and knocked over a trinket dish.

Flor rushed to them immediately, gripping them firmly on the shoulder to keep them from falling. 'Maxim. What's the plan?'

'We're leaving.' For the first time since meeting them, Maxim sounded shaken.

Maya couldn't take it any more. She rushed out of the bedroom, pushing Aga aside as she bounded down the hallway. She heard a dull thud and a grunt from Aga behind her.

'What the tak?' Nacio remarked, dumbfounded as Maya walked straight past him back into the kitchen. 'I thought I told you to lock the door!'

Maya ignored him. 'Who was that?' she demanded. The babaylan barely spared her a glance as they ran around the apartment, packing everything they could into canvas bags.

'Who was that woman, Maxim?' Maya kept up with them, deciding to follow Maxim around the kitchen. 'Why didn't you help her?' They said nothing in response, their eyes darting around the room to look for anything else to carry.

'Maya, you need to calm down.' Flor stood in front of her, blocking her from following Maxim any further. 'We'll explain in time. Just trust us.'

'Trust you?' Maya asked, incredulous. '*Trust you?* You're just a bunch of strangers ordering me around! I don't have a single reason to trust any of you!' She took a step back. 'I'm leaving. I don't understand what's going on, but I'm sure the police will.'

They would help her. They would rescue her from this insanity, and they would find Hanan. Maya could feel her breath shallowing out. This was too much.

Flor's jaw clenched. 'You're not going anywhere.'

Maxim appeared behind Flor, fear clearly etched on their face.

'That was no woman,' Maxim said as they pushed Flor gently away and took three steps towards Maya, forcing her to back up into the dining table. 'That *thing*,' they pointed frantically towards the front door, 'knows who and where we are. It's not going to leave us alone until it kills us, or at the very least takes us alive, so we need to leave. *Right now*.' Maxim stood up, slinging their completely stuffed canvas bag over their shoulder. 'I was hoping to have a few more hours of rest before I transport us again, but I'm afraid we've run out of time.' They glanced up at the ticking wall clock hanging above the bedside table. 'Flor, If I pass out on the other side, make sure I don't hit my head.'

Maya clutched at her chest. It was getting harder to breathe.

'Maya?' Aga was standing in the hallway and rubbing at his eyes, his glasses pushed up on to his head. 'Are you okay?'

Maxim's words sank in.

That was no woman.

Another brisk knock sounded at the front door.

The entire room paused. Maxim's eyes widened before they put a single finger up their lips. *Quiet,* they mouthed to everyone.

A knock sounded on the door again. 'Maxim Aganad?' A male voice with a heavy Astyrian accent called out. 'This is Astyrian patrol.'

Maya turned to Maxim, who was frozen in place with their ear angled towards the front door. No one moved as silence filled the room, save for the ticking of the wall clock.

Another knock. 'We know you're in there.'

Maya looked at Maxim in a panic. 'What are we gonna do?'

Maxim put up a finger to their lips, shushing her. *Listen,* they mouthed.

'We're looking for a young man named Agatzuki Kaneko.' The man struggled with pronouncing Aga's foreign name. 'Kiruvian male, around six foot two, black hair with glasses. Maybe you've heard of him? He's been missing for twenty-four hours. His father filed a report yesterday.'

Maya watched the colour drain from Aga's face.

'Oh, gods,' Aga covered his face with his hands as he whispered to himself, 'no, no, no.'

'A witness claims they saw you two together with a young woman named . . . Mayari Halili.' There was some shuffling on the other side of the door. 'We have the witness in our custody.'

'Ate?' Hanan's hesitant voice sounded behind the door. 'Are you in there?'

Maya felt her heart stop.

Hanan. They had Hanan.

She took a step forward. Her entire body was being pulled towards the front door, towards her sister.

Maxim held up their arm to stop her, an insistent shush leaving their lips. They pointed to their ears again, begging them to listen.

'Ate,' Hanan's voice called out to her, her name ending in a choked sob, 'are you in there? Please open the door.' A frantic knock sounded on the wood.

'Hanan?' Maya called out quietly, her body still pushing against Maxim, her feet insisting on carrying her towards the front door.

A hand immediately clamped around Maya's mouth, pulling her further away from the front door. Despite his thin frame, Hawi held her firmly in place with one arm. He held Aga's wrist in his other hand.

'What do you think you're doing? Let her go!' Aga ripped his wrist free from Hawi's grip and pulled at her shirt.

In that moment, the mess of thoughts in Maya's brain quieted, save for one.

She had to get to Hanan. Nothing else mattered.

'It's not her,' Hawi whispered angrily. 'Don't fall for it.'

She had to save her sister, and she would let no one get in the way.

She wiggled her face free from Hawi's large palm and clamped her teeth around it as hard as she could.

'*Tak*!' Hawi screamed, letting go of her. 'She bit me!'

'Hanan, it's me!' Maya called out. 'I'm here!' She dropped to the floor and crawled quickly away from Hawi, who was still clutching his hand in pain.

'Maya, wait!' Aga ran after her, clamping a hand down on her forearm to try and hold her in place. 'Just wait a second!'

'They have her, Aga!' she screamed back at him. 'Let go of me!' She pushed him back with her entire body, sending Aga sprawling on the floor. 'I have to save her!'

The rest of the babaylan sprang into action around Maya, but it felt like everyone was moving in slow motion.

Maxim's eyes glowed a brilliant white as they thrust their hands towards the floor, a white portal opening right in front of Maya. She leapt across the floor, narrowly missing the next one that Maxim opened up behind her. Flor ran to grab her, but Maya was short enough to evade her long arms, twisting away and sliding across the wood. Alon threw water balls at her back, soaking her and forcing her to her knees right in front of the door. She didn't stop.

She could feel the adrenaline pumping hard in her veins, along with a voice deep down that whispered *save her, save her, save her.*

'Ate!' Hanan called out from the other side. 'Thank goodness, you're safe.' She sobbed. 'I haven't heard from you all day. Open the door and let's go home.'

Maya's hand was already on the doorknob.

'Maya!' Maxim called to her frantically. 'That's not Hanan!' The babaylan all rushed towards her.

Maya gave the knob one twist before she paused. She took in a deep breath, allowing a split second for the adrenaline to settle and clear her mind.

Hanan never called her *ate.* Hanan always teased her that their two-year age gap didn't matter. She always called her Maya.

She released the doorknob and took a step back.

Now that she thought about it, Hanan would never approach the Astyrian patrol for help. She would rather die than ask the Astyrians for anything.

Everyone around her ground to a halt. Maxim quickly pulled her away, gripping both her forearms.

'Now you've done it,' they snapped at her.

'Mayari Halili, we know you're in there. Open this door,' the Astyrian soldier's voice commanded.

'*Ate!*' Hanan shrieked, her voice thinning and rising in pitch, the knocks becoming more insistent.

Nacio stood behind Maxim, his voice panicked. 'What do we do?'

'*Ate!*' Hanan continued to scream, her knocking turning into full-on banging. The impact shook the floorboards of the apartment.

Maya turned to face the babaylan behind her. Fear was written clearly across all their faces.

What exactly was behind the door?

Flor doubled back towards the kitchen, reached behind the refrigerator and pulled out a long whip. She uncoiled it with one swift flick of her wrist, the tip of the whip hitting the wood with a resounding strike.

She reached her free hand under the dining table and pulled out a large bolo knife still in its black leather case. She hurled it across the room towards Maxim, who caught it easily with one hand. They drew the bolo from its case, and it immediately began to pulse with a soft white light.

'Maya! Maya!' Hanan's voice was changing now, her honeyed voice turning into a high-pitched screech.

In the kitchen, Alon opened a drawer and pulled out a rusty kitchen knife. He swung it once, twice in the air before giving it a nod of approval. He took a few steps towards Aga and held it out to him without a word.

'He wants you to take it,' Hawi spoke on Alon's behalf. 'You'll need it.'

Maxim's eyes glowed to life, the white light matching the illumination of the bolo knife. 'It's too late to run now. Everyone, get in position,' they called over their shoulder. 'Bathala be with us.'

The banging on the door got even louder. On the other side of the door, the thing impersonating Hanan let out a chilling cackle. It began a taunting chant of Maya's name.

'MAYA! MAYA! Come out, come out!'

A chill ran down Maya's spine.

'Maya,' Aga called out from behind her. 'Get behind me.'

Maya scrambled back, tripping on her own two feet before moving back on her hands and knees further into the apartment.

She made it five steps before the front door burst open.

'Maya!' Aga screamed for her, just as a clawed hand grabbed her from behind and pulled her hard, slamming Maya's face into the ground. She managed to flip on to her back before the hand pulled her towards it again.

Maya heard the babaylan around her yelling at the sound of more footsteps entering the room, but her eyes focused on the monstrosity crawling on top of her.

Its face was obscured by its long, sticky black hair, its pale skin a sickening grey colour. A long, tapered tongue lolled out of its mouth, salivating. The only thing Maya could see in between the black strands was its wide, fanged smile and red eyes.

'Maya! Maya! Maya!' it chanted, the horrible, garbled version of a woman's voice as it pressed Maya further into the floor. Humongous bat wings splayed out behind its gruesome face, flapping to keep its body alight. Maya waited for its legs to pin her down, but she felt nothing past her torso. She looked down at the monster's body, only to see that it was missing its entire lower half, its entrails hanging and dripping blood onto Maya's legs.

Maya had only ever heard of monsters like these in her mother's stories. Beautiful women by day, bloodthirsty vampires by night. Demons that feasted on corpses and unborn foetuses. And now, it would feast on her.

She squeezed her eyes shut as the sound of her mother's voice reverberated in her memory.

Be careful of the mananaggal.

Chapter 22

Maya clawed at the manananggal's face with all her strength. The monster's detached body continued to hover over her, its entrails sliding all over her torso as she lifted a fist to punch at its face. It quickly dodged her fist with a cackle before pinning her arms on either side of her head. Maya aimed a kick at its body, only for her knee to connect with the air.

'Maya!' she heard Aga call out, followed by the sickening crunch of bone.

She screamed. The manananggal on top of her continued to laugh.

The sound of struggles continued around her as her brain raced to find an opening. Something heavy landed with a thud beside her, but she was too scared to look.

'Aga! Maxim!' she called out to them, but her voice was drowned out by the yells and grunts of everything around her.

The manananggal leaned in closer until its red eyes were an inch away from Maya's face. 'You thought you could hide, child of Kaylahon?' It giggled, a dark gurgling sound that made Maya sick to her stomach. 'She sees all. And she will always find you,' it sang in a sing-song voice.

Maya pressed her eyes closed as she continued to push the manananggal away. Her mind raced through old memories of nights with her mother and the stories she used to tell.

'What happens if a manananggal tries to eat me?' a young Maya cried as she clutched tightly around her mother's thigh. It was late at night, and they were standing in the kitchen after dinner. Lola Cora had just regaled her and Hanan with a story about their next-door neighbour whose baby disappeared after a manananggal attack. Hanan had laughed at the story, but Maya was terrified to go to sleep.

'I won't let that happen, anak.' Marikit ran a comforting hand over her daughter's curly hair. 'I promise.'

'But what if?' Maya insisted. 'What can I do to defend myself?'

Marikit laughed. 'Of course you'd want to fight a manananggal.' She pulled Maya into the kitchen and hoisted her up to sit on the counter.

'You won't win in a battle of strength or speed with a manananggal,' her mother said. 'You can only be prepared.'

She tapped a gentle finger on young Maya's nose. 'They say that the babaylan *had a special weapon for them called the buntot pagi. It was a long whip made from the tail of a giant stingray and blessed by the gods. They say the sound alone will drive them crazy.'*

'But I don't have that!' Maya huffed. 'What am I supposed to do?'

Marikit shook her head in amusement before pulling a jar off the kitchen shelf and placing it in front of Maya. 'My grandparents said that salt always does the job. Their entire lower half is an open wound. Throw this at them and they're as good as dead.'

'Your deaths will only be the beginning,' the monster whispered in her ear, interrupting her thoughts. 'Once you're gone, this realm will be *ours*.'

The monster unhinged its jaw and opened its mouth wide. Maya froze as she watched its tongue slither out of its black hole and slowly descend towards her face.

Her upside-down reflection in the manananggal's eyes mirrored her look of fear.

The manananggal's tongue grew longer until its tip touched Maya's forehead. Then, the wet muscle slowly wrapped itself around Maya's face. It circled twice around her, dripping black saliva onto her skin. Maya kicked and clawed even harder, pulling at the wet tongue around her, but her hands slipped each time.

The monster's tongue knocked against Maya's lips, forcing them open. Maya pressed her lips together, shaking her head from side to side.

With one strong push, the mananaggal's tongue was inside Maya's mouth, forcing it open and traveling further down her throat. She choked as the tongue slowly cut off her oxygen.

Maya knew what happened next. It was aiming for her organs. It would shove its wicked tongue down into her body and rip it apart from the inside out. It would feast on her flesh. It would bathe in her blood.

The manananggal erupted in a victorious screech as it pushed its tongue down deeper.

Maya squeezed her eyes shut, the pain of the manananggal's tongue in her throat overwhelming her.

She was going to die tonight. She would not survive this.

'Maya!' she heard a faint voice call out from behind her.

Aga.

Her eyes flew open as a pair of footsteps thundered towards her. The manananggal's eyes were glazed over, focused solely on her and the feast it was about to have.

She felt the cold bite of metal slide beneath her hand. She quickly closed her fist around it, feeling for what it is.

A knife.

At that moment, a strange sense of calm descended on her.

The manananggal was distracted and preoccupied. Maya pressed her eyes closed as hard as she could, steeling herself for what she was about to do next.

In a sudden surge of courage, she pulled the arm that held Aga's knife free from the manananggal's grip.

The monster's unfocused eyes blinked, confused by the interruption. One blink was all the time Maya needed.

In one swift motion, she sliced the knife through the base of the monster's tongue.

The manananggal shrieked as its cut tongue spewed black blood all over Maya. It writhed in pain on the floor, flapping its wings uselessly and splashing in its own blood.

Maya scrambled to stand up on her feet and gasped for air as she pulled herself free from the remaining limp muscle wrapped around her face.

'Maya!' she heard Aga's voice call out to her from behind. She turned to see him kneeling behind the kitchenette counter, quickly beckoning for her to move towards him. 'Over here!'

With the knife still in her hand, she dropped down to her knees and crawled to the kitchenette, her eyes focused solely on Aga's face and outstretched hand. There was a cut oozing blood above his eyebrow, but his gaze never left hers.

Faster, his eyes pleaded.

The sound of nails clicking on wood came up behind her. Aga's eyes focused on something behind her and his entire face drained of all colour. 'Faster, Maya!' he screamed, stretching his hand out even more.

Maya turned around to look. It was a mistake.

The manananggal was crawling towards her on the floorboards, now covered in its black, tar-like blood. The blunt end of its tongue flailed around its gaping jaw, looking for the rest of the muscle. There was anger in its eyes, and it was completely focused on one thing only.

It was coming for her.

Maya turned back to look at Aga. Her rival, Aga Kaneko, who had landed himself in this mess by showing her kindness. Aga Kaneko, who gave up his only weapon to give her a fighting chance against a monster that would now kill them both.

Her grip on the knife in her hand tightened.

She would not allow another person to die on her behalf.

She gave Aga one last look before turning back to the manananggal, now only a foot away from her. She pulled herself into a crouch, one hand on the floor to balance her. The next words she spoke came out like a snarl.

'You will not touch him.' She pointed the tip of her knife at the monster.

The manananggal pushed itself up on its arms and screeched at her, unable to speak because of its blunt tongue. It writhed and jerked as it crawled towards Maya, the same way a dying animal moved before its last few breaths. It lunged at her.

'What if I don't have any salt?' Young Maya whined at her mother. 'I can't carry a pouch of salt with me everywhere I go. People will think I'm strange.'

Marikit pretended to ponder before smiling at her daughter. 'Decapitation. Works every time.'

Maya felt an invisible tug at the hand that held the knife. She gripped the handle tightly.

The spirits were urging her to finish the job, and Maya was ready for it.

The manananggal closed in on her, talons outstretched to gouge her eyes out.

She closed her eyes and swung.

A splatter of wetness hit her in the eyes and mouth. Maya coughed, spitting out the tar-like substance onto the floorboards.

The monster's victory cry was cut short. She opened her eyes. Its loose head dropped to the floor and rolled away from its decapitated body.

She eyed the manananggal's head. It left a trail of black in its wake, its face frozen in mid-scream. The skin on its body bubbled as it emitted a foul-smelling steam. Maya watched in disgust and fascination.

'Maya,' Aga's voice trembled from behind her.

Maya turned around to look at him. He looked pale, but his eyes were bright and trained only on her. 'Please.'

Maya scrambled towards the counter, resting her back on the wood for a moment. She felt Aga's warmth as they pressed together behind the counter.

'Are you okay?' Aga whispered to her, still breathing hard. His warm, calloused hand came up to cup her bloody face and turn her to face him, eliciting a quiet gasp from Maya's lips. 'Are you hurt?'

'No,' she whispered. She scanned him from head to toe, checking if he had any wounds and sighing in relief to find none. His shirt was also covered in black blood, soaked so heavily that she could see his skin underneath. His glasses were crooked to the side, and his hair was a tangled mess, but his eyes shone brightly in the dimness, and Maya was overcome by a strange, warm feeling deep in her chest.

She was so unbelievably glad that Aga Kaneko was still alive.

'Aga,' she whispered, 'thank you.' Maya realized that her left hand was still holding the bloody knife. She dropped it and pressed her hand against the one still cupping her face.

She felt Aga stiffen for a moment before relaxing into her touch. He breathed out a heavy sigh. 'There's more of them. I barely made it back here with my life.'

Maya looked at him in confusion. 'What's going on?'

Aga tilted his head towards the living room. 'See for yourself.'

Maya turned the corner to finally look at the chaos still happening around her. The manananggal hadn't come alone.

The babaylan were standing off against monsters from Maya's worst nightmares. Six aswang stood in Maxim's small apartment, their long, pointed tongues whipping the air around them. Unlike the manananggal, their lower bodies were still intact.

One of them lay dead and decapitated on the floor, its black blood seeping into the wooden boards. Maxim had one of them cornered in the hallway with the bolo knife to its neck. The aswang sneered at them before bolting under the knife blade in an attempt to run.

Maxim raised a hand in the direction of the aswang, eyes glowing white as a portal light swallowed the monster. They raised the bolo knife with their other hand as they summoned a portal on the other side. The same aswang stumbled out, disoriented by the light before it walked straight into the tip of Maxim's knife, its shriek dying in its throat.

Maya looked to the other side of the room, watching in horror as two of them cornered Hawi against the open window.

Hawi cowered against the open window, one hand still outstretched towards the sky. 'Please, don't hurt me,' he whimpered.

One of the aswang cackled, a horrible, grating sound that raised the hairs on Maya's arms. 'How pathetic. The ward of Anitun Tabun, inherited by this pitiful thing?'

Hawi's eyes flew open, a dark stormy grey clouding his pupils. 'Pitiful indeed.'

In that moment, thunder tore through the sky with a powerful crack, and the room exploded with light. Maya watched as a bolt of lightning shot down from the clouds and struck Hawi's outstretched arm, engulfing him and the aswang in a brilliant white flash.

'Hawi!' Maya called out to him before a powerful gust of wind blew in from the open window, knocking her and Aga over. A chorus of screams filled the room as she scrambled back to her knees. The white light receded back to its source.

Hawi loomed over the two aswang cowering before him on the floor, his arms outstretched and crackling with lightning. Storm clouds rolled in his grey eyes as he smiled maniacally.

Anitun Tabun, Maya could hear her mom's memory whisper, *god of storms.*

She watched as Hawi pointed his palms towards the aswang before him. They pulled at each other, scrambling to get away from the babaylan.

Lightning shot from Hawi's hands in one quick burst of light. Maya watched in horror as the aswang screamed and the smell of burning flesh filled the room.

In an instant, the lightning disappeared. Hawi gasped in pain, as his power crackled at his edges. He doubled over and emptied his stomach onto the floor, coughing and spitting. Maya spotted drops of red coming out of his mouth.

She quickly untangled herself from Aga, pushing herself away and up on her feet. She felt her stomach drop at the sight of all the dead bodies strewn across the apartment floor. Around her, the sounds of struggle faded into an unsettling silence.

Maxim stood in the middle of it all. Their skirt was covered in black blood. A cut on their face leaked blood onto the front of their blouse, but it didn't seem to bother them. They muttered something under their breath about blood stains and laundry, seemingly unbothered by the black seeping into their floorboards. A group of corpses lay behind them, stacked on top of one another.

Flor stood by the front door, her face hard and unreadable. The buntot pagi whip hung loosely in her right hand, covered in the same blood, though her clothes were spotless. Three decapitated bodies lay around her.

'Well,' Flor sighed as she stepped over them without a single look, rolling the buntot pagi back into a tight coil, 'that was terrible. Where are the others?'

Alon and Nacio emerged from the hallway, looking worse for wear. Alon's eyes still glowed a brilliant blue as he walked back into the living room silently. The air smelled of salt as he walked past.

He stopped in the middle of the room, careful to avoid the blood and bodies. He signed to Flor, making her cluck her tongue in reply. 'You did what you had to. You don't make a big deal out of it,' she signed back to him.

'Hawi!' Nacio rushed towards the other babaylan, who was now slumped against the wall. His clothes were sizzling, and there were huge chunks of cloth missing.

Maya's eyes met Nacio's. He had the same crazed look in his eyes, a slightest hint of red in his pupils, but it quickly faded once he noticed the fearful look on Maya's face. He looked down at Hawi, whose eyes were fluttering closed.

'Hey, hey, stay awake!' Nacio cupped his hands around Hawi's face. 'Don't fall asleep. Stay awake. Hawi!' He wrapped an arm around Hawi's frail body. He turned to look at Maxim with a desperate look in his eyes.

'He's losing consciousness. We need to get out of here.' Sparks flew from Nacio's hands, the red glow returning to his eyes.

'Calm down, Nacio,' Flor warned.

'Don't *taking* tell me to calm down!' Nacio yelled. 'It's Hawi!' He choked down a sob. 'It's Hawi.'

Maya looked away, unable to watch as the babaylan argued. Instead, her eyes drifted towards the bodies strewn across the apartment floor.

Maya counted at least twelve bodies in total. All barefoot, all with the same sickly, grey skin, and all headless. Their clothes were the same loose shirts and shorts, tank tops and wide-legged pants that every other Islander wore, now torn to shreds and stained with their own black blood.

The bodies of the two aswang were unrecognizable. They lay side by side on the floor of the apartment, completely blackened and burnt to a crisp. Steam emitted from their corpses, just like the body of the manananggal.

One of the bodies had a tattoo of a jasmine flower on its calf. The other one had a colourful yarn bracelet on its left wrist, the braid loose and the edges frayed, the obvious work of an amateur. The lingering traces of humanity on the monsters' bodies unsettled Maya.

Who were these people? Why had they allowed themselves to become these monsters? Did they choose this life, or was it chosen for them?

She quickly blinked away tears and covered her mouth to keep from heaving.

Aga stood up from his hiding place behind the kitchen counter. 'Are they dead?'

'We're fine, thanks for asking.' Maxim wiped the blackened edge of their bolo knife on their skirt. 'Good to know you're both still alive,' they spoke, their voice back to its full confidence. 'Aga, you're a natural with the knife.' Their eyes narrowed at him slightly. 'Almost too natural.'

Aga cleared his throat and adjusted his glasses. 'My father enrolled me in self-defence classes when I was young. They're very popular in Kiru.' He stole a look at Maya. 'Getting beat up on a daily basis really sticks with you.'

Maxim rolled their eyes. 'Kiruvians.'

'What were those things?' He turned back to Maya.

'*Aswang*,' Maya replied quietly. 'You don't have any of those back in Kiru?'

Aga shook his head, his eyes falling to the floor. 'Not that I know of. My father, he never . . .' he cleared his throat again. 'He didn't teach me anything about the Islands. Whatever I knew before coming here, I learned from some of our Islander house staff. And books.'

House staff? Maya thought. *Just how rich was Aga Kaneko?*

'They're creatures of evil.' Flor walked up to them. 'And there are plenty of different kinds all over the Seven Islands.' She pointed at one of the headless bodies on the floor. 'These ones are similar to that silly Astyrian propaganda story about bloodsucking humans. Vampires, they call them?'

'*Vampires*?' Aga squeaked. 'Is that why they kept asking us to let them in first?' He had clearly heard of that story.

'No.' Maxim scoffed, now with a jar of salt in their arms. They were walking around now, sprinkling salt all over the dead bodies. 'That's Astyrian foolishness. The aswang just have a flair for drama. All evil creatures do.' They stepped over the dead bodies as they continued to sprinkle copious amounts of salt over them.

Maya watched carefully as Maxim emptied the contents of their salt jar. 'Why are you sprinkling salt all over them?' Aga asked. 'That seems incredibly wasteful.'

Maxim dusted off a final sprinkle of salt on the manananggal's body before throwing a scowl at Aga. 'It's too bad you don't know many folk tales, because those stories are going to come in handy for what's to come.' They held the salt up in the air proudly. 'Also, this is my salt jar *specifically* for dealing with mythical creatures. My cooking salt is in a different jar. I'm not a barbarian.' They turned back to throw the salt jar into the overflowing tote bag haphazardly draped on the couch. 'Now, I know we're all covered in blood and still recovering from the trauma of almost dying, but we really need to go. Hawi needs time to recover.'

Nacio quickly pulled a semi-conscious Hawi to his feet, an unreadable expression on his face. Nacio's held tightly on to Hawi's torso, like he was afraid the boy would disappear into thin air.

'Wait a minute,' Aga said, 'where are we going? We just killed a bunch of people and you're just gonna leave all their corpses in your apartment?'

'*Monsters,* Aga. Monsters,' Maxim responded. 'They're not people. And yes, we will, because the salt and sunlight will take care of their corpses. They'll be ash in an hour or two.'

'They were people before they were monsters,' Maya replied quietly. 'They were turned into these things.' She pointed at the body with the yarn bracelet around its neck. 'These were real people who had lives before all of this.'

Maxim groaned, their hands paused halfway up to the ceiling. 'Maya, they're not people *anymore*. They just tried to kill us. You don't have to humanize them to stifle your guilt for killing them.'

Maya swallowed thickly, the image of the manananggal's face frozen mid-scream swimming in her mind. 'We should at least bury them,' she countered. 'It's the right thing to do.'

Maxim put their hands down with a huff and pressed their lips into a thin, angry line. 'You do not need to feel compassion for these creatures. They are working for Bakunawa, and there are plenty more out there waiting to kill you. To kill every single one of us.' They closed their eyes for a moment and clenched their fists. 'They have chased us down and cornered each and every one of us with the intention of erasing us from the living realm. We are here because every single babaylan before us suffered the same fate and did not live to tell the tale. This is our reality.' They opened their eyes to reveal their brilliant white glow. The spirit of Anagolay flowed through Maxim as they raised their hands up towards the front door. 'We cannot make the same mistake. The day we choose to humanize the monsters our ancestors fought to protect us from is the day we doom ourselves.'

A large beam of white light appeared in the doorway of the apartment before Maxim, illuminating the entire living room.

Maya watched as Nacio led a limping Hawi towards the portal without a second look. Nacio took a step into the light, pulling Hawi along with him before disappearing completely. Without another word, Alon ran a few steps towards the portal before launching himself into the light.

Flor stood off to the side, adjusting the buckle on her bag strap before sparing a glance at Maya and Aga. She let out a heavy sigh. 'Maxim is right, you know. We must protect our own.' She took three big steps and jumped gracefully into the portal, the ends of her long black hair the last to disappear.

'And who exactly is part of our own?' Maya said quietly. 'Just us? What about my family? If something bad happens to them, will you ask me to leave them behind, too?'

Maxim groaned under the strain of the portal before them. 'Now is not the time, Maya. Let's talk about it on the other side.'

'Is this how it's going to be, Maxim?' she raised her voice above the loud thrum of the portal. 'You give orders, and I'm expected to follow? Will you make me give up everything else, too?'

Maxim blinked, their eyes still glowing white. 'No, Maya. I'm not going to ask that of you. That's not how this works.'

'Then promise me,' Maya demanded, 'promise me you'll let me hold on to what I can before I do this for you.' She clenched her fists. 'Promise me that my family will be kept safe from all of this. And promise me that I won't have to give up my life or my humanity in the process.' She took a step towards them. 'I may be the heir of Kaylahon, but I'm not a babaylan just yet.'

Maxim pressed their lips together for a moment, then sighed. 'Fine, I promise. No harm will come to your family; we'll make sure of it. And you can do . . .' they trailed off, their upper lip raising ever so slightly at the sight of the bodies on the floor, '. . . whatever it is you want with those things. I don't agree with any of it, mind you. You have five minutes.'

'Thank you,' Maya breathed out. Slowly, she moved towards the middle of the room and knelt on the floor, the hard wooden boards cutting into her skin. She closed her eyes, willing herself to go back in time, to a day that she had tried very hard to forget.

'I can't.'

'Danilo,' Lola Cora whispered under her breath, 'you must.'

'I can't do it.' Maya's father trembled as he stood underneath the mango tree in their backyard, his face pale as their neighbours waited for him to start the prayer.

Maya shifted uncomfortably under the pitying looks and patronizing stares of her neighbours. It had been a year since their mother was taken by the Astyrians, and neither their father nor Lola Cora had any luck trying to find her or get her back.

Their family stood in front of their community; a picture of their mother displayed on a small table set in the middle of the grass.

'She could still be alive,' Danilo muttered under his breath. 'We'd have performed a burial ritual for nothing.'

'Danilo,' Lola Cora's voice was tired, 'we've talked about this. It's time we stop pretending. It's been over a year, and we still haven't found her. Let us pray for Marikit's soul, wherever it may be, and make sure that she is guided to Kalangitan.' Her voice broke at the end. 'Let us give her the peace she deserves. That we all deserve.'

Danilo stared back at his mother for a few more moments before his shoulders slumped in defeat. 'Fine.'

Hanan sniffled beside Maya, her free hand clutching at the hem of her dress. 'What's going to happen now?'

Maya squeezed her little sister's hand. 'We're going to pray for Nanay.'

Maya took a deep breath and pressed both of her palms on the blood-soaked floorboards before her. It had been years since she last performed the ritual, but her memory of the old Hiwagani melody remained clear in her mind.

She opened her mouth to sing.

The sun sets and the shadows rise
On where our fallen warrior lies
Bathala, let their spirit take flight
Into the dawn and endless light

Tala, we pray for you to light the way
Lead not our fallen warrior astray
Haik, we pray for waters calm and wide
To carry our warrior on peaceful tides

Magwayen's river, we pray you show
Our fallen warrior where to go

Anagolay, we pray for you to send
And lead them to their journey's end

May their ancestors take their hand
To Kalangitan, the promised land
Bathala, we pray you grant them paradise
The land where spirit never dies.

When she finished, Maya felt her entire body go slack. A sob escaped her before she could stop it, and her eyes flew open as she clutched her hands to her chest. She felt the wetness on her cheeks, stunning her into silence. Her left hand reached up to touch the tears racing down her face.

She felt a gentle hand on her shoulder. Aga stood beside her, a soft look on his face. He gave her shoulder a squeeze. 'Are you all right?'

'I . . . I don't know,' Maya stammered.

'Hey, it's okay,' Aga said as he knelt beside her. He took her trembling hands in his. 'Everything's okay. You're okay. You did it.'

Maya didn't know what to say. 'What do we do now?'

'Whatever you want.' He gave her a small smile. 'I'll go wherever you go.'

Against her own will, Maya smiled at him. 'Okay.'

Behind them, Maxim cleared their throat. They already had one foot through the portal, two giant bags strapped to their torso. 'Done? Let's go.'

'Where are we going, Maxim?' Maya asked.

They looked over their shoulder at her, and their gaze softened. They extended their hand towards Maya. 'Come and see.'

Maya walked towards the portal and took hold of Maxim's strong, firm hand. She looked back at Aga and offered him her own, which he took immediately, clasping her hand tightly and squeezing it three times.

She closed her eyes as Maxim pulled them both through the light, the darkness and silence of the apartment giving way to the cool light of the moon and the sound of waves crashing against the shore.

Chapter 23

Aga pressed his eyes shut as he entered the white light of Maxim's portal.

The smell of rust and salt was in the air, and his shoes scuffed against the rough sand beneath him. He opened his eyes.

They were on an elevated dirt road overlooking the sea.

A haphazardly built fence and a collection of jagged rocks underneath their feet were all that separated them from the crashing waves below. Aga spotted the thick forest of mangroves jutting out from the underbelly of the cliff, their branches casting dancing shadows on the water. The orange hues in the sky coloured the steadily rising tide a deep purple, and for a moment, all Aga could do was watch as the world painted itself for the evening. A flock of sandpipers flew out from the mangroves, soaring above their heads and back down to the tiny strip of sand hidden in between the rocks.

He'd never been to a beach before. If they weren't running for their lives, Aga would've loved to sit by the shore and take it all in.

He looked down at his hand still tightly clasped with Maya's, her tan skin turning gold in the setting sun. The blood on her cheeks and neck had dried to a dark maroon. Her eyes were still closed, and her face was crumpled inward in anticipation.

'You can open your eyes now.' He gave her hand a gentle squeeze.

She slowly blinked once, twice, before her eyes focused on the view in front of her. 'Oh,' she breathed out, her eyes widening at the sight of the waves. 'Where are we?'

'Santa Sofia ferry dock.' Maxim had already let go of Maya and was now shaking the sandy soil out from their sandals. The rest of the babaylan stood near the fence, gazing out at the sea. 'The ticketing line just opened up for the last high-speed ferry to Saginanun, and we're getting on it.' Maxim gestured for everyone to follow them. 'Let's go.'

Aga knew little about the mysterious northern island, apart from the fact that it was cold and covered in fog most months of the year. It was the least populated island in the country, but the few residents it still had were rumoured to practise ancient Islandic rituals, some of which involved eating human flesh. The Astyrians were too scared to set up anything more than a ferry dock a few years ago.

'If there's a place where we can lay low and throw Bakunawa off our trail, it's Saginanun,' Maxim continued to speak as they led the group towards the ferry dock by the beach. 'It's the one place where we can practise our craft without fear of exposing ourselves.'

'They say the original battle between Kaylahon and Bakunawa took place along its shores,' Hawi piped in, clearly feeling much better.

'What about the people of Saginanun? They don't think it's strange that a bunch of people are walking around with elemental powers and glowing eyes?' Maya snuck a look at the other babaylan, who were trudging silently beside one another.

Flor spoke this time. She turned to look at them, facing away from the sunset and allowing the fading light to bathe her dark skin in a halo-like glow. 'The members of the Hand have been protected by the Saginanuni for centuries. The rest of the world may have stopped believing in the Old World beliefs and rituals, but they never did. They've helped us hide from the Astyrians and monsters alike.' Her eyes hardened. 'It's hard to tell the difference these days.'

Maxim interrupted their conversation with a satisfied clap. 'The last evening ferry takes Abulug Pass, so we'll make it there in less than an hour.'

Maya's brows furrowed. 'Why couldn't you just open up a portal on Saginanun instead?'

Maxim smiled apologetically. 'Since we're not yet bound together by a Kaylahon heir, there are limits to our powers. One or two calls to our gods is what we can manage in a day. Opening a portal from that distance now would burn me out, especially after what we just went through.'

'Oh' was all Maya said to that.

They walked in silence towards the ferry dock, their footfalls making soft crunching noises on the dirt road. Aga looked down to see that Maya's hand was still in his, warming up his palm and sending a current up his arm.

The blood instantly rushed to his cheeks, and he coughed in surprise.

Maya looked towards him in alarm, squeezing his hand in response, only for mortification to draw on her face a second later. Her mouth opened and closed, trying to come up with something comprehensible. She must have decided it wasn't worth the effort, because she ripped her hand out of his all of a sudden, crossing her arms in front of her and turning her gaze towards the approaching dock. Aga fought the surprising hurt that lurched in his stomach.

He knew what this was. They had just survived a life-threatening situation. Perhaps they were no longer at each other's throats, but nothing else. If circumstances were different, the thought would have never crossed his mind. *That's just what this is,* he assured himself. *Circumstance.*

So why did he feel the disappointment bubbling in his chest as they continued to walk towards the dock in silence?

They stopped at the edge of the dirt road. The rest of the way to the ferry was a steep set of stairs that led to a floating waiting shed. A long line of people snaked around the barricades, all waiting for the next boat.

Beside them was a pair of wooden toilet stalls. The stench of dirty water and something else that Aga didn't want to think about wafted towards them, making his insides churn.

Maxim pointed at the stalls. 'We're going to have to change into some clean clothes before we board. No one's going to let us ride the ferry covered in blood.' They dug into one of their tote bags and started pulling out handfuls of clothes. 'You can choose which ones you want to wear. I'm sorry I don't have anything plain.'

Hawi, now able to stand on his own two feet, immediately lunged for the plainest-looking blue polo in the pile on the ground. He gave it a good flick before holding it up for inspection. 'Not sure I can do any of Maxim's clothes justice, but at least they're clean.' He tugged gently at Nacio's holey shirt. 'Let's go before they start hogging the bathroom stalls.'

Without so much as a glance, Nacio quickly snatched the first piece of clothing off the top of the pile and hurried after Hawi towards the stalls. Maya turned to him with raised eyebrows, a look of understanding passing between them.

Flor stepped up to stand beside them. Her voice lowered as they watched Alon sign to Maxim that he didn't need any new clothes. 'Let's give them some space. Every close encounter we have could be our last, and it takes a toll on them mentally. They're just too stubborn to admit it.' She placed her hands on her hips as her gaze followed the pair. She sighed.

'Our lives are not for the weak. The gods and spirits chose us, but the human body isn't built to hold this much power for long. It takes a toll on us all. What happened with Nacio earlier, and what happened to Hawi with the aswang? That's just the beginning.'

'It gets worse?' Aga asked. He snuck a look at Maya, who averted her gaze.

Flor nodded. 'Much worse. It starts off simple enough, a pinching pain in the chest or stomach, short periods of losing control.'

'And then?' Maya pipes in, her voice hard, an unreadable expression on her face.

Flor shrugged. 'Then it starts getting harder to block out the gods' and spirits' voices in your head. Sometimes you're not . . .' she knit her eyebrows together, 'sometimes it's hard to tell if it's really you or them in your head. They take over, and you just . . .' Flor paused again. 'You're not you any more.'

'How do you know all of this?' Maya was upset now. 'You seem totally fine. Why are Nacio and Hawi losing their grip on things?'

Flor shook her head. 'I try not to call on Dumakulem as much as possible, despite being his ward. The more we do it, the easier it is for them to take over. Many babaylan before us have lost their lives that way. Most don't make it past forty.' She wrapped her hands around the amulet resting on her chest. 'We have ways of managing the symptoms.' She raised the amulet, and it immediately started to glow with a faint green light. 'Our mutya keeps the gods at bay as long as we're wearing them. The spell only lasts for one moon cycle though, so we need to harvest a new one every night of a full moon.' She lowered her mutya gently back down. 'The ones that fall out of banana trees are the strongest ones. We tend to a garden back in Saginanun, but we haven't been back in a while.'

Aga watched as Nacio and Hawi emerged from the bathroom stalls, looking much calmer and cleaner than before. He noticed the lifeless mutya around Nacio's neck, and the faintly glowing one around Hawi's. 'Nacio's mutya isn't glowing any more,' he noted.

Flor sucked in a sharp breath. 'Yeah. He missed the last full moon.'

'Is this because you haven't been bonded to a Kaylahon heir? Is there a way to stop it?' Maya pressed.

Flor paused. 'No. Even after we bond with you, it'll be the same. We'll have full access and control of our powers then. It will probably get worse.' She stared straight ahead of her, unable to meet their eyes.

'I see.' Maya's voice was hard and cold. 'I'll go ahead and change now.' She quickly snatched a colourful dress from the pile of Maxim's clothes and walked to the bathroom stalls without another word.

Maxim stood up from their squat on the ground. 'She's as brave as her mother, but just as soft-hearted.' They placed a hand on Aga's blood-soaked shoulder. 'This is hard on her. I'm sure you can talk to her about it.'

'I'm sure I don't know what you're talking about,' Aga muttered. He grabbed a random shirt from the pile and walked towards the one other empty stall, holding his breath to block out the smell.

He imagined Maya in the stall beside him, having to avoid all of the unidentifiable wet spots on the ground. Before he could stop himself, a flash of tan thighs and dimpled knees flew through his mind, sending a tidal wave of heat across his skin that pooled in his chest. He imagined her cheeks flushed pink with effort, her full lips slightly parted as she pulled the clothes over her. Aga found himself wondering if they felt as soft as they looked.

No! he scolded himself. This was the worst possible time to think about anything even remotely related to Maya. He cursed his body for betraying him.

Aga let out a sharp exhale before pulling his blood-soaked shirt over his head, finally shaking all thoughts of Maya Halili out of his mind.

Chapter 24

'Green is not your colour.'

Maya stifled a laugh as Maxim narrowed their eyes at their green polo on Aga's body. His pants still had flecks of dried blood on them, but he had washed away all the blood on his face and wiped his glasses. He had wet his hair a little bit, which was now pushed back to reveal his forehead.

He looked better. Maya hated to admit it, but he looked *handsome*, despite the green washing him out. She buried that thought deep in the recesses of her mind.

Aga's lips pressed into a straight line. 'Well, it's not like I had a choice in the matter. Last I checked, it was either this or a bright pink daster.' He looked down at his new outfit and sighed.

Maya scoffed. 'It's not like you could've pulled off the daster look anyway. The pink would've washed you out even more.'

Aga looked back up to meet her eyes, the corner of his mouth pushing upwards. 'You're right. It looks much better on you.'

Maya blinked, heat creeping up to her cheeks as Aga stiffened at his own words. He pressed his lips together to stifle a smile. Maya turned away before he could see her smile back.

She walked faster to catch up with Maxim, who was now fumbling for something inside their giant tote bag. 'Let me just bring out my purse so we can purchase the tickets. I know I threw it in here somewhere.'

They made their way down the narrow stairway towards the dock, the metal creaking and swaying with each step. The waiting shed was occupied by a long line of people snaking around the barricades, all waiting for the next ferry. Maya spotted children holding on to their mothers, their eyelids fluttering in an effort to stay awake in their tightly wrapped woven blankets. Men in construction vests were leaning against the support pillars, their heads thrown back against the metal, staring off into space. A few teenagers with heavy leather satchels stood in line, silent as their gazes travelled far past the horizon. She wondered if they were thinking about home.

The ticket master stopped mid-sentence as they descended down the steps, his eyes immediately narrowing at the sight of them. He was a stout, red-faced Islander, his skin tan and leathery from years by the sea. He wore a white sando underneath his official high-speed ferry vest.

Maya gave him a polite nod, hoping to get him to look away. The man only narrowed his eyes even more, saying something to the staff beside him before hopping off his chair and walking into the room that served as the makeshift dock office.

They shuffled in silence to the very back of the line, giving noncommittal nods to the other passengers. They looked like an odd group, a mismatch of people from all over the Seven Islands in colourful clothing.

Maxim pushed past their group to be the first of them in the line, muttering under their breath about rising ticket prices. Behind them was Alon, standing eerily still in the middle of the line, his hood still pulled over his head. Maya found herself standing behind Hawi and Nacio, who stood in comfortable silence with each other. She noted the way Nacio rocked from side to side while leaning against the railing, pressing his shoulder against Hawi's each time they got close. Aga stood right behind her, his arms crossed as he surveyed the dock.

Flor was last in line as she leaned against one of the support banisters of the dock roof. She closed her eyes and let her head fall against the wood as they all settled to wait.

Now that there was nothing but silence around her, Flor's words repeated themselves like a chant in Maya's mind.

Our lives are not for the weak.

Maya's life had been in danger more times in the past twenty-four hours than in her entire twenty-one years of life. Looking at the babaylan, she couldn't imagine how much they had lost and suffered in exchange for the lives they lived, or the lives they saved. They had proven to her that the Old World magic was real, that monsters existed, and that her mother's bedtime stories weren't make-believe folk tales for a child's imagination.

And her mother? Her mother had lied to her.

Marikit Halili had been more than just their village captain in Hiwaga. She had been the heir of Kaylahon, and she had kept that part of her a secret from Maya until her grave.

Did her father know? Did Lola Cora know?

The betrayal stung more than Maya imagined it would. For the first time in her life, she had the sinking feeling that perhaps she didn't know her mother after all.

Beside her, Hawi cleared his throat. 'You all right?'

Maya huffed out a laugh. 'I could ask you the same thing.'

Hawi's smile crinkled the corners of his eyes. 'I'll survive. The others have been doing this longer than I have, and Anitun Tabun is notoriously difficult to communicate with.' He flicked a finger at the paint peeling off the railing. 'Something about his mood changing like the weather.'

'How long has it been since you . . . ?' Maya waved a hand at Hawi, wincing at her own awkwardness. 'Has it been long since your initiation ritual?'

'Two years, give or take. I inherited the wardship from my older brother, Ipo.' His smile turned brittle. 'He's dead.'

'Oh.' Whatever she was expecting, it wasn't that.

The growing pit in her stomach deepened. Of course, it made sense the wardship of the babaylan was passed on by death. That was the only reason she was here instead of her mother.

'How did he die?' she asked quietly.

'Like all of us do, eventually. Our father passed away when we were young, and Ipo took on the wardship when he was only twenty-one, like you. He was probably one of the longest recorded wards of Anitun Tabun in babaylan history.' He paused. 'He got used to it. The others tried to warn him about pacing himself, but he didn't listen. He was calling Anitun down too much, and all of that power got to him.'

'Flor said our bodies weren't made to handle that much power. What did it do to him?' Maya pressed on. She knew it was probably wrong to keep asking, to make Hawi talk about this while in line for a ferry boat, but she couldn't resist. She needed to know.

'He called down Anitun one last time and offered his body as a permanent vessel. He was addicted to the feeling of power, they said. He didn't want to be without it.' He paused again. 'They couldn't let him go on living, the way he was in the end. He was a hollow shell of himself. He was hurting people. Ending it was the more merciful choice.'

'Hawi, I'm so sorry.' She whispered before placing her hand gently on his forearm. 'I can't imagine how difficult it must have been for you and your family.'

Maya could, actually. She knew exactly what it was like to lose someone you loved to power beyond her control.

Hawi shrugged. 'I've made my peace with it. Ipo was a great brother, but he was a terrible babaylan. He was a lot older than me, so by the time I realized what was happening, he was already half gone.'

'Did he know any of the others?' She snuck a glance at the babaylan around them.

'Maxim warned him so many times to slow down, but he couldn't. He didn't *want to.*' His voice took on a hard edge.

'Maxim was close to him?'

'Maxim loved him.' His stormy grey eyes met Maya's, shining against the harsh dock lights. 'They were together for ten years until Ipo lost it. Maxim was the only one who understood what had to be done.'

Maya stared back at Hawi, understanding dawning on her. She turned to look towards the back of line, where Maxim was still counting talukap in the palm of their hand. Under the fluorescent bulbs, Maxim looked much older, lines of weariness etched in between their eyebrows and across their forehead. Maya watched as they counted, their fingers shaking slightly as they dropped a few pieces back into their palm, cursing under their breath before starting again.

How long had Maxim been keeping the Hand together until she came of age?

He bumped against her gently on the railing. 'I can see the terror in your eyes. You look just like me on my first day.' He chuckled. 'Believe me, I know what it's like to be thrown into the fray without a single clue about what to do. My family never expected me to be the next ward, so they never trained me. It was always supposed to be Ipo.'

'But how did your family know that it was going to be him?'

'My family has held the wardship of Anitun Tabun for generations. My father, and my grandmother before him, and my great-grandmother before her. A legacy bloodline, they like to call it.' He laughed bitterly. 'Some legacy.'

'But I saw you in Maxim's apartment.' Maya leaned in closer and lowered her voice. 'You called lightning down from the sky! It was amazing!'

Hawi ducked his head and smiled. 'It comes with practise, and not without its consequences. When you finish your initiation ritual, we'll all be bound and stronger than ever, and it'll be a lot easier to train you. You've also proven yourself more than once in the past few hours that we've known each other. I think you'll be fine.'

Maya felt the knot in her stomach loosen a little. Hawi's eyes pulsing momentarily with a soft light, before turning to face the ocean. A cool breeze brushed past them, sending goosebumps down Maya's arms. She smiled, knowing where it had come from.

Over Hawi's shoulder, Nacio had wandered off to the side, humming quietly to himself. He had his back to them, but she could see how his head was turned slightly towards their conversation. She caught his eye and smiled, hoping to warm up to him. Nacio's eyebrows immediately furrowed as he turned away, pushing his hands into his pockets as he took a few steps forward in the line.

Hawi turned back to look at him and sighed. He leaned in to whisper in Maya's ear. 'You'll have to forgive Nacio. It takes a while for him to warm up to strangers, ironically enough.' The look on his face was apologetic. 'Maklium is particularly volatile, especially around water, and so is Nacio.'

'You know I can hear you,' Nacio called over his shoulder.

'That was the point,' Hawi deadpanned.

'I don't hate water,' Nacio grumbled. 'But Maklium does.'

'God of fire?' Maya offered. Again, she offered a silent thank you to her mother for telling her every single old Islandic folk tale before bedtime as a child.

Nacio shrugged. 'Occupational hazard.'

'Does it bother you?' Maya asked. 'Not being able to stand being around water as much?'

Nacio turned around, pursing his lips. 'A little.'

'Nacio used to be a competitive swimmer back in Uma,' Hawi announced proudly.

Nacio smiled. 'Yeah. A long time ago.' His eyes took on a wistful look.

'The beaches in Uma are beautiful,' Maya nodded. 'We used to go there for day trips during the summer.'

'They're still beautiful,' Nacio replied, though his smile was quickly fading. 'I just haven't swum there since . . .' he trailed off, then caught himself. 'I don't really swim any more.' He looked so defeated in that moment that Maya reached out a hand to him, thinking of giving him a hug or a reassuring pat.

Instead, Nacio turned around and moved in front of Hawi, stepping away from Maya and ending the conversation.

Maya quickly pulled her hand back, the sting of rejection painting her cheeks red.

Of course, she thought, *these people aren't my friends. They brought them with me because they need me.*

Before Maya could ask any more questions, a loud voice called out at the very front of the dock. 'High-speed ferry leaving for San Fernando, Saginanun, eight o'clock! Prepare your residence cards and bags for inspection.' The ticket master was back in his high chair, waving a green flag in the air to signal that the ticket booth was now open.

Slowly, the line of people came back to life. It was a slow shuffle towards the front as people showed their residence cards and bags to dock security.

Maya reached into her pant pocket, only for her to touch the billowing fabric of her borrowed pink daster.

She paled. Her residence card was supposed to be in her pocket.

Right. She changed out of her pants earlier in the bathroom stall. She'd have to go back up and get it.

'Do you have your residence card on you?' She turned to Aga, unease starting to creep up her throat.

'Of course.' Aga looked at her, confused. 'I always have it on me.' He pulled out a worn leather wallet from the back pocket of his trousers, opened it and pulled out a thin, worn-out piece of cardboard. 'You don't?'

She looked down at Aga's residence card, which listed all of his personal details. *Agatzuki Kaneko*, it read. *Date of Birth: 01 May. Place of Birth: Yamanomoura, Koumyou Prefecture, Kiru. Nationality: Kiruvian. Height: 189 cm. Weight: 80 kg.* She memorized the details and stored it in the back of her mind.

'I'm pretty sure I have it in my pants pocket, but I left them in the bathroom stall up there.' She pointed up towards the cliff. 'I'll go back and get it.'

'Be careful,' Aga warned. 'Make it quick.'

Maya could feel herself smirking. 'Are you worried about me, Kaneko?'

'Yes, and?' Aga replied, straight-faced.

Maya blinked. 'Okay. I'll be quick.' She quickly stepped past Aga before he could see the heat creeping up her cheeks.

After a string of muttered apologies to the others in line, Maya made her way back up the rickety dock steps, careful to avoid the holes where the rust had eaten away at the metal. She finally stumbled over the last step into the darkness, retracing her steps back to the bathroom stall.

Fortunately, it didn't seem like anyone had used it since she had changed out of her bloodied pants. She immediately spotted it on the floor, though it was in a much soggier and smellier state. Maya held her breath as she picked it up with the tips of her fingers, careful not to let it touch her skin. She laid it out on the sandy ground outside and patted it down, feeling for the outline of her residence card.

Maya's heart dropped as her hands skimmed over the smooth fabric. There was no outline of her card in any of the pockets.

That was impossible. It was supposed to be in her pocket. Astyria had required all native Islanders to carry a residence card with them at all times for identification and travel from island to island.

Except she hadn't travelled outside of Kinadman in months. The last time she did was when she and Hanan went back home to Hiwaga for the holidays. She left it—where had she left it? All she remembered was that she had stopped bringing it to work because she left it in a lecture hall once, and it had taken weeks for her to get it back.

Maya wracked her brain for the latest memory of her holding her residence card, something, anything, even just a fleeting glimpse of it. But her mind drew blank.

A creak on the metal stairway made Maya whip her head around. Aga stood in the darkness, his silhouette outlined by the harsh lights below. In the shadows, Maya could make out a frown on his face. 'What's wrong?'

'I can't find my residence card.' She shook her head and laughed, though she found nothing about this situation funny. 'I don't . . . I don't remember where I last put it.'

Aga bit his lip. 'That's okay. It happens. Do you have any other identification on you? University ID maybe?'

Maya shook her head. 'I don't have anything on me.'

Aga cursed under his breath. 'All right. Then let's tell Maxim and the others. I'm sure they'll think of something.' He offered his calloused hand to her.

Maya felt the heavy sigh in her chest start to ease. She reached for Aga's hand, only for her to reel back in surprise at the sound of screeching tires in the distance. She yelped, putting her hands over her ears at the sudden, unpleasant noise. Aga was at her side in an instant, placing his hands on top of hers, pressing them gently against her ears. The noise continued, getting closer and louder by the second.

The squeaky sound of rubber against metal raised the hairs on the back of Maya's neck and sent unpleasant shivers down her back and arms. She had always despised loud sounds.

She looked up to see Aga with his jaw clenched, his eyes focused on something far off into the darkness and reflecting an all too familiar emotion. *Fear.*

Maya followed Aga's line of sight and squinted into the darkness. The evening shadows had almost completely engulfed the surrounding mangrove forest a level below them, save for their roots. The knotted wood usually rose above the water, twisting around each other like a den of snakes, though the tide had risen enough for most of the roots to be submerged. But that wasn't what glinted in the dark. She heard them before she saw them.

An army jeep, kicking up gravel and sand as it barrelled down the path, making a beeline towards the ferry dock.

'Oh, tak,' Aga whispered.

Maya felt all the blood drain from her face.

Astyrian soldiers.

Chapter 25

'We need to go right now.'

Aga felt Maya stiffen in fear at the sight of the Astyrian army jeep. He counted three pale faces in the shadows, laughing at something one of them said.

'Let's go, Maya,' he whispered. 'We need to warn the others.'

He pulled at her forearm, careful to lead her down the metal stairs without letting her feet fall through the holes.

'Maxim!' he called out to the babaylan as he ungracefully elbowed his way back into the line, earning him glares from the other passengers. 'We have a problem!'

'What?' They turned around, a talukap hovering midair above the stack in their palm, clearly irritated by the interruption. 'Where have you been? We're almost at the ticket booth.'

Aga pointed up at the raised earth frantically. 'Astyrians.'

Maxim's face paled as their talukap clattered to the floor. 'Tak.'

Alon, who had been hunched over against the railing behind Maxim, immediately straightened, the hard look clear in his eyes replaced by a brilliant blue pulse of light. He signed something to Maxim, who nodded in agreement. 'Alon's right. I don't know what a troop of Astyrians are doing at a ferry dock this late at night, but it can't be good for us. We need to board the ferry right now.'

Hawi, Nacio, and Flor came to stand around Maxim, clearly overhearing their instructions. 'What's our plan?' Flor said.

'No matter what happens, we are getting on that ferry.' They pointed at Maya. 'Maya, most importantly. Do not let anyone stop her from boarding.'

'What about the Astyrians?' Nacio asked, his eyes coming to life with a crimson glow.

'Do not engage with the Astyrians at all costs. It's probably just a routine security check, but if they try to get in your face, you keep your head down. Clear, Nacio?' They looked pointedly at the ward of the fire god.

'What are they even doing here?' he muttered.

'*Clear,* Nacio?' Maxim asked again, this time with an edge to their voice.

Nacio grumbled in agreement before turning away. Hawi nodded at Maxim silently, following Nacio with a hand slung around his shoulder. Flor stood up straighter, crossing her arms and scowling.

'This is odd, Max. Why do they need a security check for a ferry dock at the very edge of the city? Something's not right.'

Aga's mind replayed the last conversation he had with his father in rapid motion. He hadn't revealed where they were going, hadn't even mentioned where he really was. Kenji wasn't around to report about his whereabouts any more. This couldn't be his fault. *Right?*

'The ticket master,' Maya whispered frantically. 'He was eyeing us earlier when we arrived. I saw him go inside his office for a bit, then come out again right before the ticket booth opened.' Her face paled. 'What if it was him?'

The metal stairway behind them creaked under the weight of slow and heavy steps. The chorus of voices along the dock faded into silence.

Three Astyrian soldiers descended the stairs, their light hair plastered to their foreheads and their pale skin blotchy from the humidity.

The first Astyrian came down from the steps with a hard thud, his black leather boots squeaking loudly against the wood. His black sunglasses reflected against the harsh bulb lights, casting his face in gruesome shadows. The other two hung back on the stairs, looking at him expectantly. Aga spotted the collection of gold medals glinting on the soldier's chest, and the gun holstered to his side.

Not just a soldier, then. Lieutenant, maybe. What was an Astyrian lieutenant doing at a ferry terminal at this hour?

'Good evening, Islanders,' the soldier boomed across the deadly silent dock, his thick Astyrian accent rounding out the vowels of his Kinadmani. To Aga's trained ears, he sounded like a drowning owl. It was absolutely atrocious by Islander standards, but no one was going to tell him that. Not now.

Aga took a quick look around at the faces of the Islanders around him. Save for the babaylan, not a single one looked up to meet the Astyrian's eyes. Their faces were grim, their hands clasped tightly around each other, as if bracing themselves for the worst.

'I'm Lieutenant Brigham,' a gruff voice called out from the very front of the line, 'and we're here as responders to a call made from this dock office.' A gold canine glinted in his mouth as he smiled.

The ticket master bounced down from his high chair and waved at Lieutenant Brigham, as if he knew the man personally. He waddled his way to the very back of the line, a small pocketbook resting on his big stomach.

'Good evening, sir!' The ticket master bowed dramatically to the Astyrian. Aga scoffed. Bowing was something Kiru and the Seven Islands had in common. The Astyrians never practised it. In fact, they made fun of it.

'Thank you for making time to come all this way, sir! We are very grateful to you, sir!' The man spoke in stilted Astyrian, his thick Islander accent hardening each vowel. He kept bowing, so much so that his white sando was rolling up his protruding stomach, exposing his belly button. 'You answered my call so quickly!'

Ah, Aga thought. *So, it was the ticket master.* He felt Maya and the babaylan seething beside him.

'Yes, yes, no need for pleasantries.' Lieutenant Brigham waved at the ticket master dismissively. 'What did you say your name was again?'

'Edgardo!' The ticket master replied, his voice going up an octave. 'Edgardo Matibak, sir!'

Edgardo held out his worn, sun-kissed hand towards the lieutenant for a handshake, who eyed it for a second, looking every bit like he didn't want to, but seemed to think better of it and grasped it tightly.

'Well, Edwardo, I don't usually make a habit of personally visiting run-down, Maker-forsaken ferry docks.' The two soldiers behind Brigham snickered at the obvious jab. Edgardo's smile stayed plastered on his sweaty face. 'But when the main ferry office patched your call through to our unit, I just so happened to be on a dispatch jeep with my men. I thought I might as well come down and see things for myself.'

Edgardo's smile widened. 'Of course. I know how very important the Astyrians work to keep our islands safe.' He was still holding on to Brigham's hand, shaking it faster by the second.

Maya scoffed quietly beside Aga. 'Safe isn't the word I'd use.'

Aga's eyes darted nervously towards her. 'Not the kind of joke you should be making right now.'

'Who said it was a joke?'

'Maya,' Maxim whispered through clenched teeth, 'for gods' sakes, shut up.'

The lieutenant gave Edgardo a pitying look before yanking his hand away from the man's grip. 'Rest assured that we take reports of suspicious-looking individuals leaving Santa Sofia in the dead of night seriously.' He looked around the dock pointedly, his eyes skimming over the crowd of uneasy Islanders. His gaze landed on their group, and his smile widened. 'If you've got nothing to hide, then you've got no reason to worry.'

'Are they talking about us?' Nacio whispered angrily into their tight cluster. 'Who the tak do they think they are?'

'Stop talking,' Maxim replied quietly enough for only them to hear. 'Let me think.'

'Don't you worry, folks.' Brigham turned to face them. He was tall, even for an Astyrian, enough for the top of his military-issued hat to scrape the dock's rusted metal roof. 'We ain't here to ruin your night. We'll just be assisting ol' Edwardo here with a standard security check before y'all board the ferry.' The soldiers on the stairway moved quickly towards the crowd, the humour in their expressions replaced by something cold and calculating.

'Residence cards out!' one of the Astyrian soldiers yelled, not bothering to announce it in any Islandic language. A few Islanders standing beside him flinched at the sound of his voice. 'Empty out your bags on the inspection table. All prohibited and suspicious items will be confiscated.' The corner of his mouth ticked up. 'Those who fail to cooperate will be taken in for questioning.'

Islanders all around Aga whispered in their native tongues to each other. A Kinadmani father assured his young son that they had nothing to be afraid of. Two young Umani men exchanged confused glances as they tried to piece together the soldier's instructions. An old woman hugged the small child resting on her hip tighter, cooing in gentle Gahumi.

The soldier watched as the dock filled with angry whispers and scared murmurs. He scoffed, taking a few steps towards the nearest Islander. He pushed a finger into the face of an unsuspecting young woman, who shrieked in surprise. 'Don't you know the law? You will speak Astyrian in the presence of the Astyrian military. Native tongues are not allowed.'

'Sorry,' the woman's voice was trembling, 'I don't . . . Astyrian not so good . . .' she stumbled over the foreign language, her eyes widening in fear.

'What was that?' He held up a hand to his ear, giggling. He was mocking her, challenging her in front of an audience of her fellow Islanders.

The young woman took a deep breath. 'My Astyrian not so good.'

The Astyrian soldier pushed her back towards the line and threw his head back to cackle. Every Islander watched him in silence as his laugh echoed against the four corners of the dock.

'Oh man, that was good. You can't even understand me, can you? Pathetic Islanders.' He wiped a stray tear from his eye before turning back to his comrades. 'Gets me every time.'

The woman gripped the metal barricade; her lips pressed together in a thin line. She looked down at her feet and didn't say another word.

Anger threatened to rise in Aga's throat. Edgardo was an Islander. Why did he report to the Astyrians? He was just a ticket master at a dilapidated ferry dock. He suffered just as much as everyone else on these islands did. And yet his reverential actions, his willingness to give up his fellow Islanders in exchange for *what, exactly*?

Recognition? An opportunity to rise? He acted like he *belonged* to them.

He felt a tug at his sleeve. Maya turned to him, a panicked look on her face. 'My residence card.'

'Tak, right.' He pushed his glasses up his nose before grabbing Maxim by the shoulder. 'Maxim, there's another problem.'

'What is it now?' they whispered angrily. 'We're about to get on the gods-damned ferry already. Don't call any more attention to us.'

'My residence card,' Maya blurted out, 'I don't have it.'

Maxim's eyes widened. 'You're joking.'

'I'm not.'

'Well, where is it?'

Maya took a deep breath. 'I think it's back at home. In my apartment. In Santa Teresita.' She winced at her own words.

Maxim stared at her, unable to speak. Then, they turned their head up to the sky and groaned. 'Anagolay, why must you torment me? Why must you test me this much?'

'I'm sorry, Maxim,' Maya pleaded. 'I didn't know.'

They turned to Aga and Maya with a frustrated grunt. 'We don't have time for this. We're getting on that ferry whether you have a residence card or not.' They turned towards Alon, who watched as Maxim made a series of fast-paced signals. He nodded silently before moving past them towards the back of the line, positioning himself nearest to the dock and the open sea.

'Did you hear what that Astyrian said?' Maya whispered angrily. 'They're going to demand to see my residence card, which I don't have, and then they're going to use it as a reason to take us all in for questioning! They could kill you!' She shook her head. 'Listen, you need to leave me behind.'

Maxim raised a hand up to stop her. 'No, you listen. You're getting on that ferry, and that's final. Leave it to me.'

Maxim turned away from them and pointed at Nacio and Hawi, who were trying and failing at pretending not to eavesdrop on the conversation. 'You two. Whatever happens, make sure Maya gets on the ferry. Wait for Alon's signal. I don't need any fire or lightning, so keep it in check.'

Nacio nodded grimly. 'Got it.'

Maxim turned to Flor and nodded. 'Can I count on you?'

Flor smirked, her eyes flaring with green light. 'Always.'

'Maxim,' Maya pleaded.

'Maya,' Maxim placed their hands on Maya's shoulders. 'We are babaylan, and so are you. There's no reason to be afraid.' They turned away again, bowing their head and whispering to Flor.

Maya turned to Aga, her eyes watering. 'I'm scared.'

Aga cupped her cheek and rubbed his thumb across her tan skin. 'I know. It's okay to be scared. This is a scary time. But I'm here, and the babaylan are here.'

'I have a bad feeling about this,' she whimpered. 'Everything could go wrong, and it will be all my fault.'

'No, it won't be.' He brought his hand to her chin and lifted her face up to meet his eyes. 'Trust them, Maya. Trust that things will be fine. And if they're not, at least you're not alone.' He gave her a reassuring smile. 'You have them, and you have me. I won't let anything bad happen to you.'

The small smile on Maya's face was enough to make his heart soar. In that moment, he was willing to do anything to keep that smile on her face.

They were interrupted by a loud yelp from the front of line. They tore their eyes away from each other as shocked gasps resounded all over the dock.

An old Islander man lay on his side on the dock floor, a hand clutching the left side of his face, his belongings strewn across the wooden dock planks. Lieutenant Brigham stood over him, holding up a sheathed bolo knife. He clucked his tongue loudly at the man.

'And what do we have here?' Brigham waved the knife in the air for everyone to see.

'Please, sir.' The old man got on his knees, a bruise quickly flowering on his left temple. 'It is for my work. I am a farmer in the Tomas fields.' He clasped his hands together and bowed his head, his gaze lowered to the lieutenant's boots. The old man spoke fluent albeit heavily accented Astyrian. Aga couldn't help but wonder about the circumstances that had forced him to learn it.

Lieutenant Brigham paused. He looked down at the genuflecting old man for a moment before pulling the bolo knife out from its sheath. He pointed it at the man's forehead.

More gasps erupted from Islanders all over the dock. Some called to the man, while others shouted at Brigham in Astyrian. The other two soldiers screamed at them, pulling out the guns from their holsters and pointing it at the crowd. 'A farmer, eh? That's a real nice-looking bolo for a man who works hard in the fields.' He turned the bolo around in his grip, admiring himself in the reflection. 'Looks brand new.'

'I tell the truth!' the old man exclaimed. 'I take good care of my bolo. I sharpen it every day. A gift from my father.'

Brigham hummed in response, tapping his chin in fake thought. 'Right.'

Please,' the old man continued to beg, 'my wife is waiting for me. She is alone at home.'

Brigham looked down at the old man. 'Well, let's not keep her waiting.' He smiled down at the old man, and for a moment, the old man looked up at him with hope in his eyes.

The Astyrian pulled the bolo knife away and thrust it back into its sheath. He turned his head slightly towards the other two soldiers. 'Take him in.'

'Wait!' The old man's hands were shaking as he held them up towards the soldiers. 'Please! I beg you!'

'You know the rules.' Brigham chuckled. 'No weapons aboard the ferry.'

The man's pleas fell on deaf ears as Brigham turned away and spat on the dock floor before him. 'Parker, Hansen. Not too tight on the gag for this one, all right? We respect our elderly, after all.'

The two Astyrian soldiers grabbed the man by his shoulders and hauled him up with a sharp tug.

Some of the Islanders on the dock erupted in protest, shouting at the soldiers to stop. Others cowered against the barricades, keeping their gazes averted.

Aga's blood ran cold as they dragged the old man up the metal stairs until his screams were drowned out by the whistling ocean breeze.

Chapter 26

Maya was going to throw up.

The old man's screams echoed in her skull as Brigham screamed at the other passengers.

'Pipe down!' his voice boomed across the dock. 'Unless y'all want to end up like him, I suggest you shut your mouths and do as you're told.'

'Stay close,' Maxim whispered under their breath as they inched closer to the ticket booth.

Maya's heart pounded against her ribs. She clung to Aga's arm as she imagined all of the horrible things the Astyrians would do to her when they found her out.

Lieutenant Brigham stood with his hands on his hips at the very front, a profusely sweating Edgardo cowering beside him. The Astyrian reached up and swiftly pulled off his dark sunglasses, revealing unsettling ice-blue eyes. There was nothing warm behind them. They travelled down the line until they settled on Maya. He smiled at her.

Maya looked away as a shiver ran down her spine.

Parker and Hansen came back down the stairs with smug looks on their faces, elbowing each other and dusting off their hands. They almost looked like they were having fun. Maya's stomach churned.

'Quick work, boys,' Brigham called out to them. 'Now secure the line.'

With methodical precision, Parker and Hansen began moving towards opposite ends of the passenger line, their hands held up to bar the Islanders from moving away.

White-hot rage bubbled in the pit of Maya's stomach. They were being corralled like wild animals. How dare they? How much more could the Astyrians do to humiliate and embarrass them? What more could they possibly want?

'Keep moving!' the one named Parker yelled at them.

Soon, the soldiers would force Maya to present the residence card that she did not have. They would take her in for questioning and do unspeakable things to her. They'd single out the babaylan and throw them in jail. Everything would come crashing down around them, all because of her.

She, the Hand of Kaylahon, would be the reason why everything failed.

Maya turned back to the babaylan, who were huddled close to each other. Flor's head was bent down, her eyes closed tight. Alon stood to the side, watching intently as Maxim signed to him in frantic, panicked movements. Nacio and Hawi stood side by side, their faces hard.

A few more steps and they would be at the front of the line. The Islanders before them were already boarding the ferry, their steps rocking it slightly, creating small ripples in the water.

Maya imagined herself getting on and leaving behind this nightmare.

There were only a few people left before them in the line. A young family stood in front of them, their residence cards clenched tightly in their shaking hands. The young mother had a baby bundled in cloth strapped to her front, while the father held the hand of a small boy. He looked like he had just finished crying.

Parker grabbed their residence cards, glancing back and forth between the pictures and the people in front of them, making sure that they weren't counterfeit. The family waited tensely as Parker held a flashlight up to the residence card, looking for the Astyrian commonwealth logo hidden at the back in invisible ink. Without a word, he handed them back their cards carelessly. The mother and father bowed to him frantically, thanking him in Astyrian.

Finally, it was their turn next.

'Stand behind me,' Aga whispered all of a sudden. 'Don't say a word. Maybe they won't notice.'

'Residence cards!' the one named Hansen barked out.

Maya's stomach sank. There was no chance they wouldn't notice her.

Around her, Aga and the babaylan pulled their residence cards out and handed it to Maxim, who stacked them neatly together in a pile and held it out to Parker.

Parker snatched them from their hands, shuffling through them one by one. 'Traveling as a group?'

'Yes,' Maxim replied for them, their voice clear and confident.

Parker narrowed his eyes at Maxim. 'None of you are related.'

Maxim shrugged. 'We're friends.'

'Odd mix of friends. Says here you're all from different islands.' Parker reached out a hand to where Hansen stood beside him, scowling at someone else's residence card. Hansen looked up at them, his scowl somehow deepening even more.

'We're old friends,' Flor piped in before placing a hand on Maxim's shoulder. She stared back at Parker, as if daring him to disagree.

'What are you all doing here in Kinadman?' Hansen challenged, his side of the line forgotten as he crossed his arms and faced them.

Maya curled her hands into tight fists, her nails biting into the tender flesh. It hurt, but she focused on the pain, willing herself not to break.

To her surprise, Flor gave Parker a sweet smile. 'Catching up with each other,' she gave Maxim the approximation of a tender look, 'as old friends do. Is there a problem with that?' Maya spotted Maxim elbow Flor's side.

Parker held Flor's challenging gaze, his eyebrows furrowing so hard that they formed a deep crease in the middle of his forehead. Maya held her breath, hoping.

'Fine,' Parker relented, handing their residence cards back without another look. 'Board.'

Maya let all the air in her lungs whoosh out. She felt Aga squeeze her hand reassuringly.

Everything was going to be fine. They hadn't noticed. She took a few shuffling steps forward, eager to finally board. One by one, the babaylan stepped onto the ferry. Aga placed one foot on the loading ramp and turned around, holding out a hand to her.

An arm shot up and blocked Maya from taking Aga's hand. She yelped and took a step back as Parker and Hansen crowded her, their pale eyes piercing through her.

'And where do you think you're going?' Hansen sneered.

'She's with us,' Maxim called out from the edge of the ramp.

'That's funny.' Parker turned back to them. 'I didn't see her residence card in the stack you gave me.'

Maxim waved him off, trying to act as nonchalant as possible. 'You must've missed it, but that's all right. Everyone makes mistakes.'

Aga kept his hand outstretched towards her. 'Let's go, Maya.'

Hansen slapped Aga's hand away. 'Not so fast. No residence card, no ride.' He turned back to Maya, the sneer back on his pale face. 'Let's see it, girl.'

Maya felt all the blood drain from her face as she stared up at the Astyrian soldier in front of her.

She had nothing. No card to present, no plan to escape, and no alternative.

Visions of her mother, her face pressed against the ground by an Astyrian boot, her hair being pulled by Astyrian hands, flooded her mind.

Another set of heavy footsteps made their way towards them. Maya turned around to see Lieutenant Brigham walking their way before standing in between Parker and Hansen with a knowing smirk on his face. 'What seems to be the problem, boys?'

Parker pointed squarely at Maya's face. 'This Islander does not have a residence card, sir.'

Brigham tutted under his breath. 'Oh, my. That sure is a problem.' He turned to her with a sinister smile on his face. 'Now what's a pretty Islander girl like you doin' out here without her residence card?'

From behind them, Maya could see Maxim waving at her, pressing a finger to their lips. *Don't speak.*

Maya gulped, focusing on the grain of the floorboards before her.

'What's the matter, sweetheart?' Brigham took a step towards her. His calloused hand caught her by the chin and jerked her head up. 'That pretty mouth of yours got nothing to say?'

'No, sir,' Maya stammered.

'No explanation? No apology, even?' He narrowed his eyes.

'Nothing, sir,' she whimpered.

Brigham hummed. 'Don't look like nothing to me.' He let go of her chin and grabbed her by the arm, pulling her body flush against him. 'Looks like someone who isn't getting on that damn ferry.'

'Maya!' She could hear Aga calling to her, but his voice sounded far away. She felt her body going numb as the noises around her faded to a dull hum.

Brigham dug his hand into the flesh of Maya's arm. 'Bring this one back with us,' he spoke to Parker and Hansen. 'I think she needs a . . . closer and more personal inspection, just to make sure she's really a resident.'

Maya froze as Parker and Hansen snickered and grabbed her by the shoulders, pulling her away from the loading ramp, from Aga and from freedom.

'Get away from her!' Aga took a few running steps before his path was blocked off by Brigham.

'Sorry,' he shrugged, 'but your girlfriend here is breaking one of the most important laws in the colony of the Seven Islands: Always bring your residence card. You understand.'

Aga glared at Brigham, spitting out words in Kiruvian to his face.

'Oh, a foreigner!' Brigham cackled. 'I knew you lot were suspicious.' He gestured at Edgardo, who was watching from his high chair with a smirk on his face. He scrambled off, straightening his vest as he came to stand beside Brigham. 'You, call the receiving dock and tell them this ferry is going to be delayed. Order everyone off and tell them to line up here on the side. We need to do a more thorough inspection of each and every one of them.'

Edgardo gave Brigham a quick salute. 'Yes, sir!' He pulled a walkie-talkie out from his back pocket and punched a button. He spoke into it, ordering the ferry driver to get off first. Within seconds, the few passengers made their way back to the boarding ramp, walking down and back to the dock with annoyed looks on their faces.

Aga stood alone at the edge of the boarding ramp, his fists clenched, his chest heaving as he stared after her, desperation clear on his face.

Behind him, the loading ramp was already empty. Maya paused. Where were the babaylan?

A cold ocean breeze blew past the dock. The hairs on Maya's arms stood up.

Behind her, a collection of gasps and shouts filled the dock. Parker and Hansen stopped dragging her for a moment and set her down on the floor to look at the other passengers.

Their eyes were trained on something beyond the dock, well into the darkness. A few of them were pointing, their shaky fingers outstretched towards something in the shadows.

The sound of a baby's cry filled the deck. The Islanders were panicking now. Some of them were retreating back, leaving their places in the line and moving towards the stairway.

'Quiet!' Parker ordered. 'Settle down!'

'What's happening?' Hansen demanded. 'Why is everyone panicking?'

'I don't know!' Parker yelled back. 'I don't understand Islandic!'

But Maya did. She closed her eyes and listened to their panicked whispers.

'*Yung mga puno! Tingnan mo yung mga puno!*'

Parker and Hansen turned their eyes towards the direction the Islanders were pointing. Maya felt their grip on her slacken at what they saw. She opened her eyes and stared at the darkness.

She gasped. The Islanders' whispers turned into shouts.

The trees. Look at the trees.

'Sir?' Parker's voice trembled.

'What?' Brigham replied, clearly annoyed by the interruption. He turned to look at Parker, who had a shaky finger pointing into shadows.

The shouts of the Islanders echoed against each other in the night. One by one, over and over again, they chanted.

'Yung mga puno!' the Islanders said.

'The trees,' Parker whispered.

'What are you talking about?' Brigham walked closer to the dock's edge and leaned over, straining to get a better look.

The sun had already set, and the evening shadows had almost completely engulfed the surrounding trees, save for their roots. The knotted wood was usually submerged by the tide at this time of the night.

But tonight, they rose unusually high above the water. Tonight, against the darkness, the mangrove roots slithered and twisted against each other like a den of snakes. They crawled up the trunks and branches, gripping and coiling around them, looking for something to latch on to. They made a thunderous cracking sound as they climbed the trees they held high, until they reached the very top of the trees, their scraggly tips dancing in the breeze, tasting the air.

The roots hovered in the air for a moment longer.

'Oh, Maker,' Brigham whispered.

Then, without warning, they shot across the water, aiming right towards the dock.

Everything around Maya erupted in an explosion of sound.

'Move out of the way!' Brigham shouted before diving to the dock floor, colliding with Maya and pushing her towards the edge of the dock. Maya yelped as she landed on her left arm, her jaw cracking against the wood.

The impact of the fall reverberated in Maya's skull as she pressed a hand against her temple, the sounds around her muffling. She felt the ghost of a tug on her shoulder pulling her upwards.

Get up! the tug seemed to say. *On your feet!*

Maya pushed herself up on to her knees with a heavy groan. The sounds around her returned in crashing waves.

Everyone around her was screaming. The mangrove roots were crawling across the entire dock, wiggling their way through the floorboards, the roof, and around the barricades. Edgardo was nowhere to be seen.

Something was attacking them. *But what? Or who?*

A thick mangrove root rose over her head, and she gasped, scrambling towards the edge of the dock. She wrapped her hands around the wooden support beam, bracing herself before the roots wrapped around her.

A moment later, she felt nothing. Maya opened her eyes.

The mangrove root rose past her, its tip snaking through the air. It was looking for something.

All around her, Islanders were running, bounding up the metal stairway or jumping over the barricade and into the dark ocean water below underneath.

But the roots did not touch them.

What were they looking for?

Maya's eyes scanned the dock until she found the Astyrians. They stood at the opposite side of the dock, screaming profanities as the mangrove roots wound themselves tightly around their bodies. Parker and Hansen flailed around, pulling against the coils, but each time they pulled the roots around them grew taut, squeezing them tighter. In a matter of seconds, the two were completely covered in roots, save for their heads. A series of smaller roots began to grow, slithering their way towards the soldiers' mouths and eyes.

'Lieutenant! Help us!' Hansen yelled. He began to say something else, but his words were muffled by the root that wrapped around his mouth.

'I can't see!' Parker screamed as a root wound its way around his head, blocking his sight.

'Parker! Hansen!' Brigham was stuck in his own set of roots, his one free arm flailing around helplessly.

They climbed up his body, wrapping each of his limbs individually, before pulling tightly. Brigham screamed in pain.

'Maya!' Aga exclaimed, hooking both hands under her arms and hauling her up. 'Now's our chance! Let's go!'

'Aga, what's happening?' she yelled over the noise.

Aga's eyes shone with fear. 'It's Flor.' He looked over his shoulder towards the ferry.

Leaning against the railing, Flor's eyes glowed with brilliant green light. Her hands were outstretched and pointed towards the dock, her fingers twitching and dancing in the air. Maya watched as she clenched her jaw and splayed her fingers further apart, right towards the Astyrians. Shouts of pain erupted from them as the roots coiled even tighter.

Dumakulem, Flor had said. *God of earth.*

'This is Flor's doing?' Maya exclaimed.

'There's no time to explain! Flor can't hold it forever! We have to go!'

Aga pulled on Maya's arm as he ran down the dock, pulling her along as she limped behind him. They were about to pass by the Astyrians, who were completely covered except for Brigham. The roots were closing in on his face, but not before his pale eyes spotted the two of them.

'I knew it!' he called out, his cry of outrage muffled by the roots. 'It's her!'

They ran past him, their eyes locking on Alon, who stood at the edge of the dock, his eyes glowing blue. He gestured for them to hurry up, his face a mask of concentration. As they got closer, Alon turned towards the ferry and raised his hands.

A loud metallic groan echoed against the evening shadows, and the dock shuddered. Aga and Maya fell to their knees at the force, slamming into the wooden planks together. Maya looked up.

The ferry was slowly pushing away from the dock, carried by the waves. And at the end of the dock, Alon wound his hands in the air, propelling the waves to carry the ferry away.

'Get up!' Maxim called from the ferry's edge. 'For gods' sakes, don't just stand there! *Run!*'

Maya and Aga scrambled to stand as they watched the ferry inching further away from the dock's edge. Maya's heart sank.

They weren't going to make it.

'We need a running start,' Aga's words spilled out quickly as he pulled Maya towards him. 'We need to move back so we have enough space to do it.' He clutched Maya's hand tightly against his chest and forced her to look at him. 'On my count, we jump.'

'Jump?' Maya squeaked. 'We can't!'

'Yes, we can!' Aga yelled back. 'We have to!'

Before Maya could protest, Aga was staggering back with her in tow, right towards the beginning of the dock. The mangrove roots were still crawling across the planks. Maya stepped over them, careful not to trip until Aga pulled her close, pressing his mouth to her ear.

'Ready?' Aga asked.

Maya could only nod in response.

They ran towards the ferry.

Maya ran as hard as her injured foot allowed her, ignoring the searing pain that shot up her leg. Aga huffed beside her, not once letting go of her hand.

The sound of gunshots filled the air behind them.

Maya stumbled and turned to look back.

In the middle of the dock, Brigham hovered mid-air, his whole body covered in roots except for the right hand holding the gun from his holster. Now, he was firing directly at them.

'Brigham's got a gun!' she yelled at Aga.

'Don't slow down! Just keep running!'

Maya trained her eyes ahead of her. Flor was still at the boat's railing, breathing heavily as she willed the mangrove roots to continue holding on to the Astyrians. She cried out, her hands lowering by an inch, and the mangrove roots around them dropped to the ground.

More gunshots fired behind them.

Maxim's body was halfway out of the ferry, one hand on the railing, the other hand outstretched and ready to catch them if they fell short. Alon stood on the dock's edge, his hands working tirelessly as the waves carried the ferry towards the Abulug Pass. Maya closed her eyes.

With one last step, they launched themselves from the dock's edge and flew across the water.

Maya felt herself slam into the ferry's edge, her chest hitting the metal and knocking the air out of her lungs. She held on to Aga's hand as they grasped at Maxim's arms to steady them. Before she could grip on to them, her injured foot slipped from the ferry's edge.

She was falling backwards. Maya closed her eyes and braced herself for the plunge into the icy waters below.

Two strong hands grasped on to her forearms and quickly pulled her back with a cry before pushing her away from the edge.

She collapsed on the floor, her head spinning. She stared up at the fluorescent lights of the ferry, their vision swimming with visions of mangrove roots and pale eyes.

She was alive. A disbelieved laugh bubbled in her chest.

She couldn't believe it. After everything that just happened, *she was still alive*.

She sat up, shaking her head and laughing at the absurdity of it all. 'Are you all right?' a voice asked her. She looked up to see Hawi and Nacio standing over her, twin expressions of worry on their faces.

Maya gasped for air as she continued to laugh. 'No.'

Nacio smiled. 'She's fine.'

Hawi held out a hand to her. She grabbed it and pulled herself up, looking for Aga. She had let go of his hand when she slipped. Where was he?

'You did it!' Maxim screeched as they collided with Maya, their arms wrapping around her tightly. 'You made it! You actually made it!' They jumped up and down, a warm laugh erupting from their chest.

'We did it!' Maya jumped with them as best as she could, her cheeks aching from laughter.

Flor came to stand beside them, a smile playing on her lips. 'You guys are nuts.' She shook her head amusedly. 'Thank the gods for that.'

Alon emerged from behind her, soaking wet. For the first time, his hood was down, and Maya could finally see his face. Tawny skin, shaggy black hair and full lips. He smiled at her, then signed something to Flor.

'He thinks you're very brave.' Her smile widened.

'Where's Aga?' Maya giggled. 'Aga, we made it!' She looked around at the people smiling at her. 'And Alon thinks we're brave!' She turned around in a circle, looking at every face around her, but none of them were Aga's.

Maya's laugh died in her throat. 'Where's Aga?'

Behind the circle of babaylan, Maya spotted a figure in a green polo lying motionless on the ferry floor.

'Aga!' she called out to him, pushing her way between Nacio and Hawi. She fell to her knees before him.

Aga lay on his side with his eyes closed.

'Aga?' Maya whispered. When he didn't respond, her stomach dropped. Why wasn't he moving?

She reached down to cup his cheek. His skin was cold to the touch. Maya snatched her hand back like she had just been stung. What was wrong? Why wasn't he waking up?

She felt something warm pooling around her knees.

'Maya,' Maxim's voice carried a waning, 'don't look down.'

But Maya was already looking. Her gaze drifted down, right at the warm liquid soaking her pants and Aga's polo.

It was blood.

Chapter 27

Hanan woke to the sound of distant screaming.

The darkness pressed in from all sides, an absolute, suffocating void that threatened to drown her.

She could feel the cloth tightly wrapped around her eyes. She tried to pull it off, but it didn't matter. Her hands were tied behind her. To the back of the chair she was sitting on.

This wasn't right.

The world around her was a muffled symphony of distant sounds. The scrape of metal on concrete, the rhythmic beating of her own heartbeat.

Cold dread settled into Hanan's bones.

The last thing she remembered was walking home from the police station, thinking about Maya. Worrying about what happened to her. Then, pain.

That's right. She had turned the corner towards the street that led to their apartment building's cul-de-sac. She could see the light from the apartment's lobby.

Then, nothing but excruciating pain in her head. Everything after that was blank.

A knot tightened in her stomach. Fear, sharp and raw, gnawed at the corners of her mind.

Where was she?

'Hello?' she called out. The question echoed in the darkness, unanswered.

A bone-chilling laugh echoed back.

'Who's there?' Hanan's voice trembled.

The muffled thuds of footsteps echoed from behind her in the darkness. Each one sent a hammer blow to her heart, weighing it down the closer it got to her.

A cold, rough hand clamped over her mouth, stifling the scream that threatened to tear from her throat.

'Hush, my child,' the voice hissed. 'There's no need to panic.'

A chill ran down Hanan's spine. 'Who are you?'

'You don't know me, but I know you,' it teased, its slithering timbre making the hairs on Hanan's arms stand up. 'And I think you and I are going to be great friends after we're done.'

Hanan wrenched her face away from the hand on her mouth and bared her teeth, twisting away to get a good look at the person behind her.

'What do you want from me?' she yelled.

The voice cackled into the empty darkness. 'So inquisitive, just like her sister.'

Maya.

'Where is she?' she demanded. 'Where is Maya?' She felt tears pricking at her blindfolded eyes.

'Wouldn't you like to know?' the voice sang.

'Don't hurt her.' Hanan tugged at her restraints. 'I swear to the gods, if you hurt her, I'll kill you!'

The voice clucked its tongue. 'Silly girl, the gods can't hear you. Not down here.' A high-pitched, maniacal giggle filled the room. 'And don't worry, I won't hurt your sister. At least, not yet.'

'Where is she?' Hanan screeched, feeling the rope cut into the skin of her wrists. 'Where am I?'

The voice chuckled darkly. 'Unfortunately, your sister is somewhere safe.' The soft creak of a wooden box filled the room. 'Which is more than I can say for you.' Hanan could hear the sounds of panicked chirping and fluttering wings beside her.

'What are you doing?' She felt the panic clawing at her throat now. 'Let me out! Let me out!'

'Open wide,' the voice commanded. 'Let's get down to business.'

Hanan screamed as a hand shoved the chick down her throat.

Part III

Chapter 28

Aga was floating.

The last thing he remembered was the pain. A searing, flaring thing that entered his body with the sheer force of a speeding train. It consumed him for what felt like an eternity, before leaving behind the icy numbness that now seeped into his bones.

He remembered running. The chaos around him was overwhelming, save for Maya's hand in his. He remembered thinking that he was going to die. He remembered feeling the desperate need for Maya to live.

Panic clawed at his throat. Where was Maya?

Aga groaned, the sound echoing around him. He reached up to press his palms into his eyes, forcing himself awake. He blinked once, twice, his vision blurring before finally focusing on the swirling patterns on the rough-hewn wood of the boat. He lay on his side, his legs folded uncomfortably underneath him. He tried to sit up, careful not to move too quickly and trigger any more pain, but he was surprised to feel none.

He sat up, expecting Maya or one of the babaylan to come to see him, but he was surrounded by silence.

Why was he alone? Where was everyone?

He finally glanced up and looked around. He suddenly realized why.

He was not on the sleek ferry that he and Maya had jumped on. The wood underneath him was a simple bangka, a fisherman's boat, long and slender and open to the night sky. The water underneath was quiet and calm, and not nearly as expansive as the water they were supposed to sail on. This was a river, narrow and confining, the banks shrouded in impenetrable shadows. The dark waters swirled around the boat in silent torrents.

Aga was confused. He was supposed to be on the high-speed ferry to Saginanun. With the babaylan. With Maya. This was not where he last remembered he was.

He turned around, only to come face to face with a hooded figure.

Aga yelped, scrambling backwards on the bangka, all the way to the very front. The hooded figure remained motionless and hunched over at the back of the boat, a long oar in its hands, rowing in complete silence. From the front, the figure was barely visible against the shadows.

Who were they? What was he doing here? Did they take him?

'Excuse me?' Aga called out from the front of the boat. 'Where are we?'

The figure continued rowing in silence.

'Why am I here?' he tried again. 'Where's Maya?'

He inched closer to the silent figure. Aga couldn't make out the face obscured by the figure's hood. All he could see were the long claws biting against the intricately carved wood of their oar. He decided he wasn't interested in finding out.

Aga.

A whisper echoed through the darkness.

'Hello?' He whipped his head around, looking for the source.

Aga. Aga.

Aga's heart fluttered in his chest. The voice sounded familiar.

It sounded like Maya's.

A flicker of light appeared further down the river. It shone like a beacon, reflecting against the murky waters and shadowy banks.

Aga. Aga. Aga.

The voice was echoing from the light.

The bangka glided across the river as the hooded figure continued to row. Aga fixed his gaze on the flickering light ahead. A strange wave of calm washed over him.

He sat back down and let the hooded figure guide him to Maya.

Chapter 29

There was blood everywhere.

All over Aga's stomach, on the floor, on her hands. There was so much of it.

'Aga!' Maya screamed his name as she clutched Aga's hands in her own, desperate to feel any warmth, any glimpse of life from him.

She turned him over to lay on his back as she looked over his body, looking for the source. As soon as her eyes found the steady stream of blood on his left side, she lifted his polo up, peeling back the fabric until it revealed the gaping wound. In the middle of the exposed flesh was a silver bullet.

The sound of gunshots echoed in her mind.

Brigham's gun.

'Maxim, Aga's been shot!' She got up and turned on the babaylan, clutching the front of their blouse with her bloodstained hands. 'Save him!'

Around her, the babaylan stood still. They looked at each other, waiting for the others to speak.

Without another word, Maxim pushed her gently aside and knelt beside Aga, his blood seeping into their skirt. They examined the wound, pressing a figure into the flesh. Aga groaned, his hands flailing in the air for a moment before falling back down.

It looked worse that Maya could have imagined. The bullet was nestled deep into his flesh, right underneath the left side of his ribs. Each shallow breath he took caused a new wave of blood to flow out, covering his side, his hips, his left hand. Maya could feel the wetness running down her cheeks.

Maxim pressed their ear to Aga's chest and closed their eyes, listening. Finally, they sat up again, pulled out the hem of their skirt and ripped a large piece off.

'He's bleeding out,' Maxim said matter-of-factly. 'And if I try to remove the bullet now, he'll bleed out even faster. I don't have any tools with me, but if we wait until we get to Saginanun, we'll be out of time. He's still alive, but he won't be for long if we don't do something.' They finished ripping off the large chunk of their skirt and started wrapping it around Aga's torso. 'The best I can do now is try and slow down the bleeding.'

'How do we save him?' Maya pleaded. 'Please, there has to be a way.'

'Maya, calm yourself.' Flor knelt beside her. 'Maxim is doing all they can do.' She moved to wrap an arm around Maya.

'Don't touch me!' Maya flung Flor's arm away from her, pushing her back with all of her strength. 'Save him! Please, save him!'

'Maya!' Hawi knelt in front of her and placed both hands on her shoulders, pinning her in place. 'Get a hold of yourself! We will save Aga, but you need to calm down!'

She shook her head at him. This was all wrong. Aga couldn't be wounded. He couldn't be bleeding. Not Aga. *Not her Aga.*

'Maxim,' Flor's voice warned, 'don't. Whatever you're thinking, don't do it.'

'It's the only way.' Maxim stood up, their skirt soaked in blood.

'You'll hurt yourself,' Flor countered. 'You could die! And for what, so this foreign boy we don't even know can live?' she asked incredulously.

'If Aga dies, it will be because we put him in danger.' Maya watched as Maxim slowly backed away towards the edge of the ferry. 'I can't. I can't take another innocent life.'

'What about Maya?' Flor challenged. 'She needs you. We need you.' Her voice turned pleading. 'I need you. Max, you can't.'

Maxim's eyes came alive with a white glow. 'Once we make it to Saginanun, make sure to load me into a tricycle.'

They raised their hands up. With a deafening cry, white light shot from their palms, and the night exploded.

Maya screamed and fell over as the blast of illumination engulfed the entire ferry. She crawled towards Aga and threw herself on him, desperate to protect him. When she realized that there was no pain, she opened her eyes.

Around her, the night sky and sea were gone. Instead, a perfect, luminescent white landscape stretched out before her. At the very back of the ferry, Maxim stood tall, their hands raised up, their eyes completely flooded with white light.

'Maxim, what have you done?' Hawi cried.

Slowly, the white light swallowed the tip of the ferry, inch by inch until it completely engulfed the first half of its body. Maya gasped.

Maxim had opened a portal big enough to transport the entire ferry.

'Everyone, hold on!' Flor yelled over the metallic groan of the ferry.

With one last scream, Maxim threw their head back, light exploding from their eyes, their mouth, their arms and legs.

Maya clung to Aga, holding his hand and praying for a miracle.

The ferry surged forward and disappeared into the white light, leaving nothing behind but froth on the waves.

Chapter 30

They emerged on the other side of the light, the misty shores of Saginanun welcoming them home.

The ferry buckled as it landed back in the water, rocking back and forth as it found its balance. Maya held on to Aga, her panicked tears staining his chest. She turned around to look at Maxim, just in time to see them collapse on the ferry floor.

'Max!' Flor cried, running to their side. She pulled them into her arms, cradling their head in her lap. 'Nacio, Hawi, flag down the dock workers. Use the code.' She pressed a finger to the side of Maxim's neck and waited for a beat before releasing a sigh of relief. 'They're alive.'

Maya let out a relieved sob. She couldn't believe what Maxim had done. They had pushed themselves to the very limits of what a babaylan could do to give Aga a fighting chance at survival.

'Maya,' Hawi called to her. She turned around and looked up at Hawi, who knelt down beside her. There were storms in his eyes.

'Listen to me.' Hawi's voice was quiet. 'As soon as we dock at Saginanun, you need to do the initiation ritual. With Maxim unconscious and Aga bleeding out, we can't afford to wait any more.'

'I don't understand,' Maya stuttered out. 'I thought I needed to train for it.'

'You do, but there's no time. If you do the initiation ritual tonight, your spirit will be sent to Kalangitan and you can finally bond with the gift of Kaylahon. If Aga's on the brink of death, you could find him there. You could guide him back to the world of the living. You could save him.'

'Can't we bring him to a hospital?' she demanded.

Hawi shook his head. 'We can't. Bakunawa has eyes and ears everywhere. We can't take any chances.'

'Can't you heal him?' She looked at the babaylan standing around her, their faces solemn. 'Can't you call down your gods and save him?'

'We cannot,' Flor spoke. 'None of us can. Our gods don't heal. They only destroy.'

'But you, Maya,' Hawi said, you could. You're the Hand of Kaylahon. You hold the most power among all of us. If there's anyone who can save Aga, it's you.'

Maya felt her heart shatter. This was all her fault. If it weren't for her, Aga wouldn't have had to save her. He wouldn't have been shot trying to get her on the ferry. And now, he was bleeding to death. Because of her.

Maxim was unconscious on the floor, drained of power. Because of her.

'I'll do it,' Maya whispered. 'Tell me what I have to do.'

'We have to bury you,' Flor said, 'in a trunk, underground. Alive.'

'The spirits will take over when you're on the brink of death,' Hawi said. 'Your consciousness will travel to Kalangitan, and if you survive, the spirits will send you back.'

'I'm sorry,' Maya blinked, 'did you say bury me alive?'

'Yes.'

'I'm not doing that.'

'Yes, you are.' Flor pressed two fingers at the crease forming in between her brows.

'Are you insane?' Maya shook her head one more time, the knot in her stomach tightening. This late at night, the fog surrounding the outer banks of Saginanun shielded most of the shore from view. *They were so close.* 'I'm surprised none of you died in the process.'

Flor narrowed her eyes. 'Yeah, well, so were we. This isn't a game, Maya. The ritual happens this way for a reason. Between the five of us on this boat, you're the only one with the strongest ties to the spirit world. If you don't do this, Aga dies.'

She looked down at Aga's unconscious form beside her, lying eerily still on the floor of the boat. She took his cold hand in hers and gave it a squeeze, willing him to open his eyes.

Please, she begged. *Live.*

As soon as they got near enough to wave at the San Fernando dock workers, they immediately jumped into action and docked their ferry within minutes. The Saginanuni left them to their own devices and stayed out of their way for the most part, some of them even offering the babaylan sips of water from their own metal flasks.

'Do they know what you—*what we*—are?' Maya asked.

Nacio shrugged as the ferry shook with impact. 'You'd be surprised how many Islanders grew up with the stories of the Old World and its magic. They were told stories by their parents, who were told stories by their parents, like my family.' He glanced quickly at Hawi, who was speaking in hurried Saginanuni to a dock worker. 'You know what they always say. Islanders never forget.'

Flor scoffed as she slung Maxim across her back and lifted them up like a ragdoll. 'Some of them do. And when they do, everyone around them suffers for it.'

Maya thought about Edgardo at the ferry dock. Edgardo, the ticket master, a fellow Islander who had willingly reported to the Astyrians, who had bowed to them and had done their bidding. Who sacrificed his countrymen for a chance at recognition.

And now Aga was suffering because of it.

She balled her fists. *Never again*. She would become a babaylan, and she would never let another person she loved suffer ever again.

'Let's move quickly,' Hawi instructed. 'We'll carry Aga down the boat. You call a tricycle for us. Just tell the driver, *bulutong tubig*.'

Maya raised an eyebrow and was prepared to object, but she thought better of it. She swallowed her pride and bound down the unloading ramp, already waving at the line of tricycle drivers parked at the transport shed beside the dock.

'Bulutong tubig!' Maya cupped her hands around her mouth as she yelled at the nearest tricycle driver. 'Bulutong tubig!'

As she took a deep breath and prepared herself to yell again, a tricycle driver at the very front of the line revved his motor engine and zipped his way to the very edge of the road, right where Maya stood.

The driver said something to her in Saginanuni, pointing to his right at the sidecar attached to the motorcycle he sat on. On any other island, Maya might have been able to understand a little of what the driver was saying, but the Saginanuni language had developed differently from the other islands, making it the most unique-sounding of all the seven. She had no idea what he was talking about.

'Sorry,' Maya said in her Kinadmani, raising her hands up apologetically and hoping he understood.

'Ah.' The driver paused for a moment and cleared his throat before continuing. 'I can carry all of you. Some can ride in the sidecar, some behind me on the motorcycle, and others can just hold on to the roof,' he said in thickly accented Kinadmani and smiled.

'Oh.' Maya blinked in surprise. 'All right.'

The sound of heavy footsteps walking down the unloading ramp made Maya turn around. Hawi, Nacio, and Alon held Aga tightly as they brought him down from the boat, their faces betraying the strain they were under. Flor followed right behind them, carrying an unconscious Maxim on her back. The tricycle driver quickly moved to help them, placing Aga and Maxim side by side in his passenger car.

'Maya, you and I can sit behind the driver on the motorcycle,' Hawi said as he gave the tricycle driver more instructions in Saginanuni. 'The others can ride on the roof.'

Maya yelped as Hawi pushed her onto the main motorcycle, squeezing her against the back of the tricycle driver. Flor, Nacio, and Alon stepped on to the back of the motorcycle with one foot and grabbed the passenger car's roof, hoisting themselves up onto the surface. Nacio lay flat on his stomach, his arms holding tightly to either side of the glinting metal. Alon braced himself on the railings attached to the sidecar. Behind her, Flor clung to the metal grills behind the motorcycle, one foot on its taillight and the other on the wall of the sidecar. She banged on the roof with her palm three times. 'Step on it!'

With one last rev of his engine, the tricycle driver sped away from the dock and into the foggy Saginanun night.

Chapter 31

Maya wasn't quite sure what she imagined the babaylan's place to look like, but it definitely wasn't what stood in front of her. Her imagination had painted pictures of a secret lair, a hidden cave or a labyrinth of mystical, pre-colonial tents with apprentices and assistants welcoming them home.

Instead, the tricycle driver sped through the main road, passing by lush forests of jungle foliage on the left and the Seventh Sea on the right before skidding to a stop at the end of a dirt path, in front of a very normal-looking old house that looked like it had been built decades ago during the Marinese era.

The bottom floor was made of concrete and had no other openings save for the tall, wooden door in the middle, while the second floor was made of wood and had large windows that wrapped around the entire house on every side. Underneath each window were the traditional cooling vents that residents opened on especially sweltering days to let the hot air out. The home had seen better days, but it seemed well-kept. Maya wondered how the babaylan found any time to maintain such a place.

The five of them made quick work of unloading their unconscious passengers out of the tricycle sidecar; Flor with Maxim, and the remaining four of them with Aga. Before he left, the tricycle driver said something to Flor in Saginanuni. He placed a hand on his heart and gave her a deep bow.

She paused, Maxim dangling over her back, before she raised a hand over the man's head and uttered something under her breath. The man smiled, bowing one more time before turning back to his tricycle.

'What did you say to him?' Maya asked as she braced both hands under the weight of Aga's right leg. 'And why did he know exactly where to go just from "bulutong tubig"?'

'I gave him a blessing on behalf of Dumakulem. He needed help with his crops.' They turned back around to watch the tricycle kicking up dirt and dust as it drove away. 'It's the least we can do for the Saginanuni after all they've done for us.' She grunted under Maxim's weight as they made their way to the front door of the house. 'Generations of Saginanuni have served the babaylan. We've come up with shortcuts to let them know what we need in emergencies.'

Before Flor could raise her fist up to the wood, the door swung open, revealing a tiny old woman in a colourful floral daster. She adjusted her round spectacles on her nose and strained her neck upwards at them.

Flor's hand hovered in midair as they regarded each other in silence. Maya could feel the tension in the air as she eyed the babaylan beside her, waiting for her to say something.

'Manang Nella,' Flor's voice was strained, 'help.'

The old woman's eyes narrowed at them for a moment before she scoffed. 'Clear out the dining table. Place the boy on top,' she grumbled as she turned around and padded back inside the house. 'Bring Maxim up to their room. They need to rest.'

Maya swore she felt the babaylan heave a collective sigh of relief as they toed off their shoes and entered the house.

Maya looked down at Aga, whose eyes still remained closed. She could still see the faint rise and fall of his chest, but the time in between each breath and the next was getting longer each time. His face had taken on a pallid hue, and the blood soaking his clothes was spreading. *Please*, she begged the gods, the Maker, the universe, anyone who cared to listen. *Please let me save him.*

'This way.' Hawi pulled gently on Aga's left shoulder to guide them towards the dining room. 'And welcome to Kubli.' He smiled weakly. 'You can thank Flor's great-great-great-great grandmother for all of this.'

'You mean that Marinese aristocrat that forced the Saginanuni of this island to be her servants? Let's not.' Flor scoffed.

Manang Nella was already putting away unused plates and the basket of fruits that sat in the middle of the table. 'Nacio, get a blanket from upstairs,' she called from over her shoulder as she rummaged through one of their cupboards. Flor bound up the grand staircase, taking two steps at a time with Maxim still on her back.

They placed Aga as gently as they could on top of the dining table, careful not to jostle him too much. Nacio disappeared up to the second floor, rushing to get a blanket. Hawi and Alon stood around the dining table nervously, eyeing his unconscious form. Manang Nella pushed up on her knees, carrying a small basket of bandages and pincushions. She stood beside Maya, looking her up and down behind her glasses.

'Hello,' Maya stammered.

Manang Nella huffed in response. 'You look just like Marikit,' she said before waddling up to the dining table.

'You knew her?' Maya asked in shock.

'Child, I raised her.' She waved her hand around dismissively. 'I raised every single one of these fools, and the fools before them.'

'Manang Nella has taken care of generations of babaylan,' Flor said as she came up beside Maya, only a little out of breath. 'Just like we are the wards of the gods, she is ours.'

Maya watched wide-eyed as Manang Nella pulled out one of the wooden chairs with a groan and knelt on the seat, pushing herself up slightly to lean over Aga. She pressed two fingers to Aga's neck, trying to find his pulse.

'His pulse is very weak,' Manang Nella said. 'He's not long for this world.'

Maya felt her stomach drop.

The old woman wobbled as she got off the wooden chair. 'I'll try my best to suture the wound, but it seems like he's lost a lot of blood on the way here. Even if I call in a favour at the island satellite clinic, it's at least an hour's ride away.' She shook her head.

Maya turned to Hawi. 'The ritual. Let me do the ritual.'

Hawi nodded solemnly. 'It's time.'

There was no other way around it. She was going to have to do the ritual. She had to do it to save Aga's life. In the back of her mind, she heard the voice of her mother from an old memory. *You are blessed beyond measure, Maya, and you will hold the sky, the stars, and the spirits of our ancestors one day if you are willing to accept them.*

Manang Nella nodded. 'The rest of you, head to the back garden and get the shovels out. It's time to start digging.'

Chapter 32

'I have to get into that?'

They were out in the babaylan's backyard, sweaty and breathless after digging the six-foot hole in the ground before them. Banana trees swung gently around them in the evening breeze, their leaves rustling against each other.

Maya eyed the empty trunk in front of her. Her throat dried up at the sight of the tiny space she had to fit herself into.

'Apologies, we didn't have any full-length coffins lying around,' Flor grumbled as she dusted off the dirt on her pants. Maya had joined them in the digging, using a rake to claw the soil away, while the rest had attacked the soil with their shovels as fast as their hands could possibly manage.

The hole was definitely wide and deep enough to fit the trunk with her inside of it. She just didn't want to think about what was going to happen when she was covered with dirt and six feet under.

'I've only ever witnessed one ritual in my entire life.' Nacio wiped the sweat off his brow, his curls sticking to his forehead. 'Hawi's was right over there.' He pointed at a spot underneath a guyabano tree growing at the edge of the property. 'And if Hawi can do it, you've got nothing to worry about.'

'Thanks.' Hawi crossed his arms and rolled his eyes at Nacio, the slightest hint of a smile playing on his lips.

Maya took a deep breath and stepped towards the trunk, flinging the top open, dust billowing into the air from years of being undisturbed in Kubli's attic.

A warm hand gripped her shoulder. Hawi looked at her, all traces of amusement gone from his face. 'Once you're in the trunk, we'll lower you down into the hole and cover you back up. When you're buried, you will start hearing the voices of the spirits. They will overwhelm you, you will probably feel like you're going crazy. You have to give in and allow them to take over. It's the only way that your soul can be brought to Kalangitan and form a permanent connection with them. *Only on the edge of death will you be granted a new life*.'

Maya nodded. She took one last deep breath and stepped into the trunk.

It was much roomier than she expected, considering that it used to hold piles of old papers. She squatted inside the trunk, her right leg pinching slightly as she tried to find a comfortable position. She tried her best to stop the panic from taking over. She had to do this. For her mother, for the babaylan. For her family.

For Aga.

She leaned back in the trunk and pulled her knees up to her chest, the hardwood biting into her back. Her eyes met Hawi's, who stood over her, his hands gripping the edge of the trunk's opening. 'Remember, Maya. This ritual is also a test. The spirits want you, so allow them to take over.'

'What happens when they do?' Maya said, her lower back straining in the position she was in.

'Magwayen, the goddess of souls, will guide you. A bright light, a boat, and a river. Remember that. There's no telling what else the spirits will show you.'

'What did they show you?' Maya asked quietly, settling further into the trunk.

Hawi paused. 'My brother.' He gave her a sad smile. 'I got to talk to him for a bit. It helped me find peace in the end.' He looked down at her again. 'I hope you do, too.'

'Thank you, Hawi.' Maya felt her eyes pricking with tears.

Hawi looked over his shoulder one last time and nodded. He looked back down at Maya. 'It's time.' He reached down and grasped her hand tightly. 'If it means anything, I'm sorry. For everything. It wasn't supposed to happen this way.' He let out a heavy sigh before releasing her hand. 'Don't die.' Before Maya could reply, he turned away from the trunk with a hand over his mouth. In his place, Flor walked into view.

'Hang in there. We'll see you soon.' She gave Maya a quick nod and the ghost of a smile before quickly disappearing from view. Maya swore she saw her bringing a hand up to wipe across her cheek.

Nacio stepped up to the edge of the trunk, his expression unreadable. Maya gave him a weak smile.

'I have to say, I didn't expect you to do the ritual so soon.' He cleared his throat. 'Most babaylan go through intense physical and mental training for months before even thinking of getting buried.' He looked down at his feet. 'For what it's worth, I hope you make it out alive. See you on the other side.' He turned around abruptly and walked away.

She half-expected Manang Nella to show up, but she didn't. Instead, she heard the sound of Flor's voice on the other side of the trunk, right behind the lid.

'Are you ready?' she asked.

Maya took a deep breath. 'Yes.'

With a loud groan, the lid of the giant trunk was slowly closed shut over her head. The last sliver of moonlight shone in her eyes for one more second, a reminder of the world she was leaving behind.

She felt the heavy lid close with a loud thud. The jingling of the lock sent vibrations into the body of the trunk, shaking Maya. A few more metallic clanks, the sound of the heavy padlock sliding into place and one last click. Then, the sound of muffled voices around her. She could just barely make out the sound of Flor's voice ordering the other babaylan to carry the trunk.

She felt the trunk lifting off the ground with a slight swing. She braced herself with a hand on either side as it wobbled, moving in awkward angles and uncomfortable positions. She could hear the grunts from the babaylan outside the trunk as they slowly carried her down into the hole in the ground.

After a few minutes of struggling, Maya finally felt the trunk land on the ground with a gentle thud. She could still hear the voices around her, but they sounded more muffled and far away now that she was down in the dirt.

Slowly, the sound of the voices gradually faded to silence. Maya could hear nothing but the sound of her own breathing.

The faraway sound of scraping overhead immediately caught her attention. Right above her, a soft pattering hit the lid of the trunk.

They were starting to bury her.

Immediately, panic clawed at her throat. She felt the small space closing in on her, and her chest started to tighten.

'Wait!' she called desperately. 'Wait, let me out!'

Her hands frantically searched in the darkness for the thin sliver of space in between the lid and body of the trunk, trying to wedge her fingers through it. She found the small crack, her eyes watering as she pressed her fingers through it as much as she could, to no avail. It wouldn't budge.

Her throat constricted in pain as she swallowed down big gulps of air. She pounded on the thick wood, her heart hammering against her ribs as she screamed. 'Let me out! I can't do it! I can't do it! I can't breathe!'

The sound of dirt hitting the trunk continued, until the voices above her, completely oblivious to her panic, faded to a distant murmur. After what felt like an eternity, they disappeared into complete silence.

The air inside the trunk was thick with the smell of damp wood. It pressed down all around her, mixing with the smell of her sweat. Each breath felt shallow and painful, like trying to breathe underwater. The darkness was absolute and suffocating. She pressed against her eyes, blurring the edges of her vision.

Maya pushed her curls away and pressed her ear against the wood, straining to hear something, anything that would break the suffocating silence, but there was nothing. Only the frantic pounding of her own heart echoed in the confined space.

She sank back into the foundation of the trunk and pressed herself against the cold, hard wood.

Maya was alone. Buried six feet underground, with no way of escaping. Alone, trapped, and utterly helpless.

She thought of Maxim, completely drained of energy and power, deciding to risk their life for Aga's safety.

She thought of Aga lying on the dining table, wounded and close to death. She pictured him bleeding out, the life draining from his eyes.

Because she couldn't do it. *Because she had failed.*

A faint sound blew past her ear. It was so soft that Maya couldn't decipher it, but she realized what it was.

Voices.

Mayari. A soft whisper blew in her ear.

She yelped, covering both ears at the sudden sound.

Mayari! A different voice called out, this one more desperate-sounding than the first one. One by one, new voices joined in until it was a chorus of dissonant voices overlapping over each other.

Help us.

Mayari!

You are too weak.

Give yourself to us.

Help us.

Stop!

The spirits were calling to her.

Only on the edge of death can we be granted a glimpse into our new life.

She was dying.

We have been waiting for you.

She closed her eyes, took a deep breath, and allowed the spirits to take over.

Chapter 33

Maya was weightless.

Her eyes snapped open as her breath caught in her throat. She felt the smooth, cold surface underneath her.

Was she still inside the trunk?

She heard the soft lapping of water against wood. Her eyes drank in the shadows that surrounded her. Everything was clothed in darkness, save for her body.

Was she dead?

She sat up with a jolt, adrenaline coursing through her veins. Slowly, the world swam back into focus. Her gaze followed the sound of the water.

She was on a bangka. Underneath her, a river flowed past, its surface dark and murky. There was no other sound save for her shallow breaths. Slowly, her memory returned to her.

She knew this place.

Her mother had told her stories about it before bedtime. This was what Hawi had warned her about.

This was Magwayen's river.

Just as she started getting her bearings, she felt the hairs on the back of her neck stand up. She wasn't alone. She turned around.

Behind her, a hooded figure sat at the very back of the bangka, running their oar silently through the waters. Maya didn't need to see their face to know who it was.

'Magwayen,' she spoke the god's name.

The hooded figure raised its head slightly, enough for Maya to see a glimpse of ocean blue eyes, jade-coloured skin, and silvery hair. Magwayen said nothing to her but instead lifted a slender hand and pointed a finger ahead of them.

She raised a hand to her chest and bowed to the god before her. Without a word, Magwayen ducked her head in acknowledgement. Maya turned around to see where she was pointing.

The river stretched on beyond what Maya's eyes could see, but at the very end was a beacon of light reflecting against the water.

'Where are we going, Magwayen?' she asked the god. 'Where are you taking me?'

Magwayen stayed silent as she rowed the bangka effortlessly down the river. Maya realized that she wasn't going to get any answers from her.

She sat and waited.

They rowed down the river for what felt like hours. As they travelled further down the river, the banks gradually widened, its dark waters receding into a deep emerald green. Each moment, the beacon of light at the end of the river got closer and closer.

Finally, they reached the end of the murky depths. Magwayen gave one strong push with her oar, and the bangka plunged into a dark cave. Maya found herself surrounded by complete darkness.

Maya shivered as she clutched either side of the boat, bracing herself for whatever was to come.

Aga, she thought to herself. *For Aga.*

At the very end of the cave, the beacon of light was blinding. Maya squinted, raising a hand up to cover the glare, but it was too much. She closed her eyes, praying that she wasn't riding to her death.

The bangka passed through the light.

In an instant, warmth touched Maya's skin. She opened her eyes, expecting to be blinded by the sun. Instead, what she saw took her breath away.

Before her was a lush valley, surrounded by mountains with peaks covered with fog. The water underneath her, once dark and murky, had transformed into a clear and vibrant blue.

At the very end of the river was a waterfall, shimmering in the sunlight. Maya soaked it all in, unable to believe her own eyes. The valley before her was a vibrant tapestry of greens and blues, dotted with the warm browns of nipa huts.

That stopped Maya. Houses. *People.*

Traditional Islandic houses covered the valley, shimmering like liquid gold under the sun. And among the clusters of houses, Maya spotted people.

Hundreds of people were milling around, strolling along the riverbanks, carrying earthen jars of water on their heads, calling to each other from across dirt paths.

'Who are these people?' Maya wondered.

'Souls,' Magwayen whispered from behind her, making her jump. So, she does speak. Maya looked closer at the people milling around by the shore, their faces shining and sun-kissed.

Every single one of these people were dead.

But they seemed so full of life. Maya spotted elderly couples lounging in front of their homes, sipping on mugs of steaming liquid. She saw children running after each other, their bubbling laughter carrying over the sound of the crashing waterfall. Maya realized where she was.

This was Kalangitan.

Magwayen quietly guided the bangka to the shore, reaching her long oar over Maya's head to stop the boat in front of the wooden dock steps. She pointed a finger at the steps and nodded. Maya took this as a sign to get off.

'Thank you, Magwayen.' She bowed to the god one more time.

Magwayen returned the bow, the faintest hint of a smile playing on her lips. She looked up, her eyes focusing on something behind Maya. For the first time, she smiled.

'Mayari,' a voice called from behind Maya.

She froze. She knew that voice anywhere. She listened to that voice every night before bed for years.

She turned around.

Marikit Halili stood before her, smiling like the sun.

'Nanay?'

Chapter 34

Maya ran.

'Anak.' Her mother's eyes glistened in the light. 'Come here.' She opened her arms wide.

Their bodies collided and she wrapped her arms around her mother.

She wept, allowing herself to release every ounce of grief and pain that had settled deep within her bones all these years. She wailed, clutching at her mother, and gave herself permission to cry until the river within her ran dry.

Through it all, her mother held her tightly, gently stroking her hair and kissing her cheeks.

'Oh, Maya,' her mother whispered in her ear, 'I've missed you.'

'Nanay,' Maya called for her mother over and over again as they held on to each other tightly. Her tears stained her mother's simple linen dress, the stain flowering on her shoulder. She realized that she was still wearing the clothes the night she was taken by the Astyrians.

Her mother was here. Her mother was safe.

But her mother was dead.

Maya wept for what felt like an eternity. The river within her was endless. Nothing else mattered but allowing it to flow.

All she knew was that she was with her mother again.

Marikit gently pulled away, running a soothing hand over Maya's cheek. 'Anak, look at you, you're all grown up. And so beautiful.' She smiled at Maya.

'I've missed you so much,' Maya cried, pressing her mother's hand against her cheek. 'I can't believe it's really you.' She choked back a sob. 'How? How are you here?'

Her mother shook her head. 'We don't have to talk about it now.' She gave her daughter a sad smile. 'I don't want to ruin our reunion.'

'No, Nanay. I need to know.' Maya took a deep breath, trying her best to calm herself. 'How did you end up here?'

Marikit paused. 'They shot me.'

Maya sucked in a deep breath. 'Where?'

'On the beach,' Marikit said, 'after I told your father to bring you inside, they shot me. Three bullets to the head. Then they burned my body to hide the evidence.' Her eyes took on a faraway look. 'They said it was payback for when I set fire to their base.'

'But did you?' Maya pressed. 'Did you do it?'

'Yes.'

'Why?' Maya cried. 'Why, 'nay?'

Marikit grasped her daughter's hands. 'Anak, I had to. They insisted that the local government unit had signed a contract saying that they could build their base on Hiwaga, but I never did! They forged my signature!' Maya could feel her mother's hands tighten around hers. 'I just couldn't. I couldn't let them do it, not after they forced their way into our land, into our homes, into our culture. They were prepared to take everything from us. I had to stop them somehow.'

'But they still built the base, 'nay.' Maya felt the tears running down her cheeks. 'After you died, they still built it.'

Marikit's smile fell. 'Oh.'

Maya continued to sob, not caring that her mother saw.

Years of her wondering what happened to her mother, only for her to find out she had died for nothing.

She died for *nothing*. Nothing but an ugly Astyrian military base sitting on the shores of Hiwaga.

'Hush now, anak.' Marikit wrapped her arms around her daughter. 'It's all right. What's done is done. I made that choice, and it is only mine to bear. It's not your fault.'

'But it is mine to bear!' Maya cried. 'I am the next Hand of Kaylahon, and it's because you're dead!'

Her mother froze. 'You're here because of the initiation ritual, aren't you?'

'How did you know?'

'Because I went through the exact same ritual all those years ago.' She leaned in close and whispered, 'you're a babaylan, just like I was.'

'Why didn't you tell me?' Maya demanded. 'I don't understand why you kept that part of you a secret. Why did you leave the Hand? Why didn't you use your powers to defend yourself against the Astyrians?'

Marikit sighed. 'Because being a babaylan is a burden that we must bear for the rest of our lives. When my mother died, that burden was passed on to me. And I was so young, anak. I didn't know how to deal with all the responsibility suddenly thrust upon me.' She sighed. 'I was given all this power, but I had to sacrifice the life that I had always dreamed of in return. I didn't want power. I wanted a family.'

'Is that why you left?' Maya asked. 'Maxim told me.'

Marikit brightened. 'You've met Maxim?'

Maya gave her a small smile. 'They told me all about you.'

'I'm so glad they're still alive. I dreaded the day I would run into them here in Kalangitan.' She breathed out a relieved sigh. 'Yes, I left. I didn't want that for you or Hanan. I wanted to live my life, with the destiny that I chose.' She shook her head. 'I guess that didn't turn out so well.'

'But now I have to,' Maya whispered. 'Something bad is happening in our world, Nanay. Bakunawa manifested out of Kasanaan for the first time in over a thousand years. She has all the monsters and demons on her side.' She sucked in a sharp breath. 'If I don't do this, the Hand of Kaylahon and the Seven Islands are doomed.' She looked down at the ground. 'I don't have a choice.'

Marikit wrapped her arms around her daughter once again. 'Anak, listen to me. Ours is a powerful gift. The spirits speak to you, seeking your wisdom, your compassion and your will. But you can choose. You can decide if this path is truly the one for you.'

Maya's eyes widened. 'But Maxim said that if I don't do this, the spirits will take over me. If I fail here, I fail everyone.'

'Then answer them,' Marikit said, 'answer their call, accept the power of Kaylahon. The spirits can demand your acceptance, but they cannot demand your obedience.' She locked eyes with Maya. 'You are a kind soul, Maya. You are brave, you are compassionate, you are strong. You can accept the call, but you alone have the power to choose your own destiny and make a difference in this world. You do not have to live the life that the Hand dictates for you.'

Maya looked down at her hands, her fingers digging into her palms. 'But that's not what the Hand is expecting of me.'

Marikit smiled, a bittersweet expression gracing her lips. 'Your duty is not to fulfil their expectations. Your duty is to yourself. To live a life that brings you joy, a life that honours your own truth. You can have all this power, live a normal life, and still be enough. You can be a loving daughter, a devoted wife, a cherished friend, and still be powerful.' She squeezed her daughter's hand. 'To be a woman is to be more. That is our gift.'

Maya looked up at her mother, her eyes filling. 'And it will be enough?'

Marikit pulled her daughter close, embracing her warmly. 'Always,' she whispered. 'You will always be enough.'

They embraced, and Marikit's warmth seeped through Maya's bones, enveloping her in a comforting heat. She pulled back, looking at her mother's face. Same curly hair, same tan skin, same brown eyes. Same heart, same will.

She would see this through.

A memory flickered in the recesses of her mind. Someone else was dead. Or dying? She couldn't remember.

Aga!

'I have something to tell you,' Maya said frantically. 'I'm also looking for someone. A friend.' She racked her fuzzy brain for the details she was supposed to remember. 'He was shot while trying to protect me, and the babaylan said he was on the verge of death.' She swallowed. 'The reason why I agreed to the ritual in the first place was to save him.'

'Oh!' Marikit exclaimed in surprise. 'A friend! What kind of friend?' Her eyebrows raised ever so slightly.

'Nanay!' Maya exclaimed. 'I'll explain on the way. But he's important.' She felt her cheeks heat up at having to explain this to her dead mother.

Marikit giggled and clapped her hands together. 'Well, then what are we waiting for? Let's go get him!' She pulled Maya up to her feet and intertwined their fingers together. She led Maya down a dirt path, flanked by nipa huts left and right.

'You know where to find him?' Maya asked incredulously.

'Kalangitan is a vast place, just as big as the Seven Islands themselves, but there are different places for different people, depending on the way they died.' She gestured to the nipa huts around them. 'This is the island for those who died trying to save others. I'm here on this island, so if your story is correct, then your friend should be somewhere here, too.'

Marikit led her up and down multiple dirt paths, waving hello to everyone they passed by. Some of them even stopped to talk to Marikit, asking her about the next fiesta, their child's health and the incoming dry season.

'Why is everything so . . . normal here?' Maya wondered.

'Kalangitan mirrors the real world,' Marikit replied, 'but in its most ideal form. Here on this island, everyone gets to live their most ideal lives in peace and harmony. It is Bathala's way of rewarding us for our sacrifice.'

Finally, Marikit stopped in front of a nipa hut at the very end of a much shorter path. She turned to Maya and smiled.

'This is where I stay,' Marikit said. 'I have a strong feeling that whoever you're looking for could have ended up here. Bathala works in mysterious ways and listens to our greatest desires. The universe makes it happen, especially here in Kalangitan.' She pushed the door open. 'Just take it slow. He's still tethered to the world of the living, so his memory is still fuzzy, and he probably won't remember anything once he wakes up.'

The inside of the nipa hut was flooded with the sunlight coming in from the open window. There was a single bed, a clay pot on top of a traditional kalan stove, and a small dining table with two chairs.

Maya gasped.

At the dining table sat Aga Kaneko.

'Aga!' Maya exclaimed as she rushed into the nipa hut.

'Maya?' Aga asked, clearly confused. He stood up from the dining table just as Maya jumped into his arms.

She wrapped her arms around his neck and buried her face into his collarbone, inhaling his familiar musky scent. Aga held her tightly, squeezing his arms around her waist. He pushed his nose into her hair, and Maya felt his lips brush against her curls.

'What are you doing here?' Aga asked, still very much confused. He pushed Maya back and scanned her up and down. 'Are you all right?'

'I'm fine!' Maya laughed as happy tears ran down her face. 'It's so good to see you, Aga.'

Aga raised his eyebrows, still not understanding. 'Yeah, you too.' He looked around the nipa hut. 'Do you know where we are?'

In that moment, Maya's heart ached for him. *Kind, smart, and courageous Aga Kaneko*. She never wanted to be without him again.

He probably won't remember anything once he wakes up.

It didn't matter. She would make him remember.

Without an ounce of hesitation, Maya pushed up on her tiptoes and kissed him.

He tasted like warmth and the salt from her tears. Aga froze, momentarily taken aback, until his hands came up to cup her face and he was kissing her back.

He pressed his lips against hers, wrapping his arms around her waist and lifting her up until her feet were off the floor. He kissed her, slow and warm and delicious, all the years of things left unsaid melting between them. Maya smiled against the kiss.

When they finally broke apart, Aga was panting, his eyes wide with a mixture of shock and disbelief.

Maya took his hand and laced her fingers with his. Immediately, Aga's cheeks flushed a deep crimson. Maya laughed. 'I do, but I can explain on the way. Let's get out of here.'

She looked over at her mother, who stood smiling in the doorway. 'Nanay, can you show us the way out?'

Marikit smiled. 'Of course. You've already been here for too long.'

'I still don't understand.' Aga scratched his head as they made their way back to Magwayen's river. 'So, I'm dead?'

'Technically?' Maya said as she swung their intertwined hands between them as they walked. 'So am I. But once Magwayen takes us back, we won't be dead any more.'

'Huh' was all Aga said.

They wound around the dirt paths, their hands tightly intertwined, swinging between them. Maya felt a small pang of guilt at the kiss. She knew Aga wasn't going to remember it. He probably wasn't going to remember anything they said or did in this place.

She wondered if he reciprocated any of the feelings she felt for him. She only hoped that he was willing to try it again when they were back in the land of the living.

Finally, they made it back to the riverbank. Marikit turned towards Maya and Aga, her eyes twinkling. 'This is it, children. Once you ride Magwayen's boat back, you'll return to the land of the living. When you get on the boat, you'll see the light. Just close your eyes.' She smiled. 'Remember this place, this feeling, for it will always be a part of you.'

Maya let go of Aga's hand and ran to her mother one last time. She wrapped her hands around her in a tight hug.

'I love you, Nanay,' she whispered in her ear. 'Thank you.'

'I love you, anak,' she whispered back. 'Remember me.'

Maya hugged her tighter. 'Always.'

They boarded the bangka where Magwayen waited quietly with her oar in her hands. Once they boarded, Magwayen slowly pushed away from the dock and dipped her oar into the blue water, paddling away from the vibrant colours and misty mountains of Kalangitan.

'Are you ready to go back?' Maya asked Aga.

'I'm not entirely sure what's happening, honestly,' Aga said. 'I have no idea where I am or who we just met.' He reached for her hand and held it tightly. 'But I trust you. I'll go wherever you go.'

The bangka neared the brightness as Magwayen guided them away. Maya and Aga closed their eyes, their hands still clasped together, as the world around them began to shimmer and fade into a swirling vortex of light. They felt a gentle tug, pulling them back towards the life they had left behind.

As the light behind her eyes intensified, Maya felt her mother's words echo in her heart.

You will always be enough.

She felt the warmth of the light consume her, and then they were gone.

Chapter 35

Underneath the light of a full moon, the soil of Kubli came to life.

Hawi jumped to his feet, nearly toppling over in the lawn chair he set up in the backyard as the ground underneath them shook.

The other babaylan exclaimed, pointing at the spot of freshly overturned dirt and watching in awe as thousands of soil particles slowly rose into the air.

It had been over eight hours since they buried her. They were still holding on to hope during the first half, but when the neighbouring roosters had started crowing to signal the early morning, they had resigned themselves to a horrible truth.

They thought she was dead.

But Hawi felt her power before he saw her.

The ground shook as a hand burst free from the soil, its palms glowing with a brilliant white light.

Hawi smiled.

She was coming for them.

Chapter 36

Hanan's head was pounding.

She opened her eyes, blinked once, and let the darkness recede in waves until it was replaced by a sickly green glow.

The cloth around her eyes was gone, but the rope binding her wrists remained, digging painfully into her skin. She was in a small, circular room, the walls slick and cold. A single, flickering bulb cast long, dancing shadows that writhed and contorted like grotesque creatures.

She tried to sit up, but a wave of dizziness washed over her, forcing her back down. She tried to remember what had happened, but her memory was a fractured mess.

All she knew was that she was *so hungry.*

Her throat was bone dry, and her tongue felt thick and heavy in her mouth. She felt the hunger awakening within her, an ugly, ravenous thing that demanded that she eat.

Eat. Eat. Eat. Eat. Eat.

Then, she noticed it. The uncomfortable sensation of her own skin. Something felt wrong.

She looked to her side and discovered a dirty floor-length mirror. She reached for it, only for her gaze to fall upon her hands. They looked different. The skin was stretched taut with the veins throbbing beneath the thin surface. Her nails were longer and sharper. Her eyes trailed to the dark appendages behind her.

Growing from her back were two leathery bat wings.

She gasped and sat up abruptly, only for her to lose her balance and fall off the metal table she lay on.

She fell to the floor with a hard thud. She pushed herself up on her arms and gathered herself to stand up, until she realized she couldn't. She looked down at the rest of her body.

There was nothing past her torso. Her legs were gone.

Hanan screamed.

Epilogue

The salt spray lashed at Lieutenant Hanzo's face as he gripped the railing of the small fishing boat.

He had been on boats his whole life. It was not his first time sailing the choppy waters of the Banahaw Sea, but that did little to dampen his nerves.

When Masaki Kaneko briefed them on this mission, he thought he was joking.

No enemy soldiers, no armies, no battles to be fought. Just whispers of the supernatural, of ancient magic, and of creatures that defied all knowledge and logic.

'Nervous, Mori-oya?' Hanzo asked the young man beside him. He was the youngest of the crew, and Hanzo could tell. His face was pale as he stared out at the setting sun against the horizon, his knuckles white as he braced himself against the waves.

Mori jumped, startled. 'S-sorry, Lieutenant. Just . . . I've never seen such a beautiful sunset before,' he stammered.

'Neither have I,' Hanzo admitted. 'But don't be fooled. The Seven Islands may be beautiful, but they are deadly.' He didn't elaborate. The less they knew, the better.

They had been traveling for days posing as fishermen, with their nets laden with fake catches. Masaki Kaneko's orders were simple: infiltrate the Seven Islands, locate his son and send him back to Kiru, verify the supernatural phenomena he reported on and report back. No engagement, no confrontations, just observation.

As they neared the archipelago's largest island, the air grew heavy. Out in the open sea, the sky was a canvas of vibrant orange hues. Now, as they got closer, it bled out into a bruised purple, heavy with clouds.

'Lieutenant,' Mori whispered, his voice trembling, 'do you hear that?'

A low, guttural growl echoed across the water, sending chills down Hanzo's spine.

Hanzo buckled against the railing. 'Alert the others.'

Mori gave him a quick salute before running below deck, shouting for the others to come up.

The growling around their boat intensified. It shook the boat, sending Hanzo's team into a panicked frenzy.

'What's going on?' Tanaka called out from below.

Hanzo felt a cold dread creeping into his bones. His eyes focused on the murky waters ahead of them.

From underneath the waves, a colossal shadow rose above the boat.

Hanzo stared into the swirling mist, his heart pounding.

The boat lurched violently from side to side as the shadow rose even higher.

Hanzo pulled a flashlight from his work belt and shone it at the shadow, squinting to get a good look at it. The light reflected back, catching against a geometric pattern of scales.

Scales. Hanzo felt his stomach drop.

This was no ordinary mission. This was a descent into the unknown.

With a deafening roar, the shadow lunged.

Acknowledgements

The concept for *She Who Devours* started years ago as a raw, unexamined idea I had when I was a college student. However, the actual motivation to write it made itself known in September 2023, after a visit to the Manila International Book Fair. I had just started making content on TikTok for the book community, and I was excited to be devouring books at a steady pace again. The world of Philippine literature is and always has been immensely rich and diverse—and after that day, I realized how badly I wanted to contribute to it. It took me another two and a half years of extensive research, writing a handful of half-assed first drafts, and questioning my self-worth before this book became what it is today. As an avid reader of fantasy myself, it has always been my dream to see Filipino folklore and mythology appreciated for its richness and diversity across the world, and it is my hope that this book contributes to that dream in its own small way.

That being said, writing a book is no joke. I would be nothing without the village that raised me and supported me. I'd like to express my gratitude for all the people who've made all of this possible:

To Nora Abubakar and the Penguin Random House Southeast Asia team, who took a chance on me and believed in my story. Thank you for working with me on this project and for giving me the opportunity to share it with the world.

To my editors, Amberdawn Manaois, Eshwari Gaddam, and Rounak Bhat, whose expertise shaped my story in a way I never could on my own. Thank you for believing in my work and helping it reach its full potential.

To Simran Singh, who guided me through the unfamiliar world of book marketing. Thank you for answering all my questions with grace and patience.

To my cover artists, Adviata Vats and Divya Gaur, who brought my vision of Maya and Bakunawa to life in such a beautiful way.

To Zoe Policarpio, my very talented friend: Thank you for bringing the Seven Islands to life in a beautiful world map on such short notice. I owe you a big hug.

To the Filipino BookTok community, who welcomed me with open arms, thank you for your love and support. You are the reason why I was brave enough to even attempt this in the first place. I promise I won't talk about my book in every single video.

To my friends Ron Tayag, Mita Del Mundo, Sofia Gagante, Virna Aguirre, and Rich Armia, for your never-ending support and enthusiasm for this book.

To Jody Uy and Brian Ramos, for giving me their time, advice, and friendship. I kept getting stuck in a prison of my own uncertainty and you helped me out of it every single time. I don't think I would have survived without you guys.

To my college English literature professor, DM Reyes, who taught me how to write, and whose class permanently altered my soul. This book is a testament to your impact on me as a teacher.

To Bianca Henares, who didn't know I was writing this book but did so much for me just by existing and being my best friend. We've come a long way from writing self-insert One Direction fanfiction. Thank you for everything.

To my family—Mama, Kuya, Tita Mench, Julia, and Jake—who have met every single one of my crazy ideas and new endeavours with nothing but unwavering love and support. Thank you for being by my side throughout it all.

To my mother, who has been and done everything a mother possibly can in her lifetime and more. Words will never be enough to express my gratitude and love for you.

And to Roy, who has always believed in me, whose patience and understanding rivals the depths of Magwayen's river. Your love has made all of this possible.